SIR FIG NEWTON
AND THE
SCIENCE OF
PERSISTENCE

SIR FIG NEWTON AND THE SCIENCE OF PERSISTENCE

BY
SONJA THOMAS

ALADDIN
New York   London
Toronto   Sydney   New Delhi

$E=mc^2$

🧞‍♂️ALADDIN

An imprint of Simon & Schuster Children's Publishing Division

1230 Avenue of the Americas, New York, New York 10020

First Aladdin hardcover edition March 2022

Text copyright © 2022 by Sonja Thomas

Jacket illustration copyright © 2022 by Brittney Bond

All rights reserved, including the right of reproduction in whole or in part in any form.

ALADDIN and related logo are registered trademarks of Simon & Schuster, Inc.

For information about special discounts for bulk purchases, please contact Simon & Schuster Special Sales at 1-866-506-1949 or business@simonandschuster.com.

The Simon & Schuster Speakers Bureau can bring authors to your live event. For more information or to book an event contact the Simon & Schuster Speakers Bureau at 1-866-248-3049 or visit our website at www.simonspeakers.com.

Book designed by Tiara Iandiorio

The text of this book was set in Sabon LT Std.

Manufactured in the United States of America 0222 FFG

10 9 8 7 6 5 4 3 2 1

Library of Congress Cataloging-in-Publication Data

Names: Thomas, Sonja (Children's author), author.

Title: Sir Fig Newton and the science of persistence / Sonja Thomas.

Description: First Aladdin hardcover edition. | New York : Aladdin, 2022. | Audience: Ages 8 to 12. | Summary: Eleven-year-old Miranium's summer is going downhill fast: her best friend, Thomas, has moved away, her know-it-all nemesis, Tamika, has moved too near for comfort, her parents are stressed since her father has lost his job, she has just blown up the microwave with an ill-advised experiment (destroying her own cellphone in the process), and worst of all her beloved cat, Sir Fig Newton, has developed diabetes; there is no money for his medical care, and her parents want to re-home him—but Mira is determined to raise the money somehow even if it means turning to Tamika for help.

Identifiers: LCCN 2021023576 (print) | LCCN 2021023577 (ebook) | ISBN 9781534484924 (hardcover) | ISBN 9781534484948 (ebook)

Subjects: LCSH: Feline diabetes—Juvenile fiction. | Cats—Juvenile fiction. | Money-making projects for children—Juvenile fiction. | Fathers and daughters—Juvenile fiction. | Families—Florida—Juvenile fiction. | Family crises—Juvenile fiction. | Friendship—Juvenile fiction. | CYAC: Cats—Fiction. | Diabetes—Fiction. | Moneymaking projects—Fiction. | Fathers and daughters—Fiction. | Family problems—Fiction. | Friendship—Fiction. | Florida—Fiction.

Classification: LCC PZ7.1.T4672 Si 2022 (print) | LCC PZ7.1.T4672 (ebook) | DDC 813.6 [Fic]—dc23

LC record available at https://lccn.loc.gov/2021023576

LC ebook record available at https://lccn.loc.gov/2021023577

In memory of Whiskey
and Bailey, and to all the
four-legged fur babies that
bring joy and connection into
our lives.

And in memory of my father,
Dalton E. Thomas. Thank you
for sharing your love of music,
animals, and sports with me.

CONTENTS

A WORLD OF SUCK

Fact: Grapes don't always explode with scientific reliability.

The microwave had stopped heating, but the little green oval halves looked exactly the same. Refusing to give up, I ignored the graveyard of dissected fruit on the countertop and plucked another from a bowl, cut it almost in half, and then placed it on a plate with five other grapes.

Even though natural plasmas are rare on Earth—other than lightning or the northern lights—man-made plasmas are everywhere. Just about everybody has seen a TV or computer with a plasma screen. I was still fuzzy on why nuking grapes could cause a plasma ball. Something to do with the microwaves trapped in the watery fruit and getting really hot. Whatever the scientific theory, I loved the idea of creating my own mini twinkling star, even if it only lasted for a microsecond.

I tried to focus on making my experiment precise, but my nose crinkled from the smell wafting in from the Crock-Pot. Dad's "chili." With Mom working so much after he lost his job, he was trying his best, but I sure missed Mom's cooking.

My cat, Sir Fig Newton, didn't seem to mind the smell. He sat at attention on the kitchen floor with his tummy sprawled out beneath him, so big that he looked like he'd swallowed a basketball, along with the whole Orlando Magic team.

I set the plate in the microwave again. My finger hovered in front of the start button. "Third time's a winner, right, Fig?"

He chattered, a cross between his dainty meow and a goat's bleat, usually reserved for when he's spotted a bird through the sliding glass door. His excitement was contagious, but before I had a chance to start the microwave, my phone rang.

I snatched my cell from my back pocket. My best friend's narrow face, almost buried under his chestnut curly shag, filled the screen in the video-call app. I grinned.

"Oh my Einstein! I was just about to do your favorite experiment."

"Hey, Miranium," Thomas replied. His wide smile exposed the gap between his top center teeth. "Exploding grapes?"

"Yup!"

"You think it'll really work this time?"

I huffed. "I *always* make it work."

"Yeah, yeah, yeah. Hey, why did the man take his clock to the vet?"

"I don't know. Why?"

Silence. Thomas wiggled his nose. I sighed, waiting for it. As always, he allowed the dramatic pause to go on way too long.

"Well?" I prompted.

"Because it had ticks."

I groaned, but couldn't mask the grin on my face.

"You'll never believe what I saw," Thomas said.

"Can't be as awesome as a grape plasma ball." I gestured to the microwave.

"The US Capitol, the Washington Monument, *and* the White House. Did you know that plans for a monument started *before* Washington was elected president?"

I rolled my eyes. Thomas was over the moon when it came to American history. It was the one teeny-tiny reason he'd been excited to move precisely nine hundred and one miles away from Florida to Washington, DC.

"Mm-hmm. Sounds neat. But did *you* know that plasma is the most common state of matter in the universe? And that stars, including our sun, are big balls of plasma—a really hot gas with lots of energy?"

"Okay, okay." Thomas chuckled. "I'm no match for your stubbornness superpower."

"Um, I prefer 'persistent.'" I held the phone out so it faced the microwave. "Prepare to be blown away."

I hit the start button. The microwave hummed. *Ten . . . nine . . . eight . . .* A bright yellow spark hissed, right at the bridge of skin joining the two halves of the grape. Another flame crackled. I snuck a glance at Fig. His proud facial response clearly read: *Fur reals, you got this.*

Five . . . four . . . three . . . Just as a third plasma ball ignited, the microwave shut off and the timer countdown vanished, along with the kitchen lights.

I slapped my forehead. All hail the Short-Circuit Scientist.

"Mira!" Dad's voice boomed from down the hall.

Fig tore out of the kitchen, and I dashed in the opposite direction. As I ran, my phone flew from my hand, smacked against the cabinet door, and skipped across the kitchen floor. No time to stop. Once I reached the laundry room, I scrambled up the ladder and flipped the circuit breaker switch twice. Electricity zoomed back on.

I hustled back into the kitchen and braked a few inches before slamming into my dad towering in the middle of the room. The microwave door hung open. A charred, sugary stench tangled with Dad's chili. Using an oven mitt, he was gripping the plate of smoking grapes.

"You know better than to do this experiment without an adult present. You could damage the microwave, or worse." He sighed. "Plus your mother would kill us both if you blew up the house."

His voice wasn't all angry. He mostly sounded

exhausted. He wore a faded purple Prince concert tee and ancient running shorts he constantly had to pull up. Tangled kinks crowned his head. Stubble tickled his chin. I called it his stuck-at-home uniform. It was all you had to wear to spend your days surfing the job ads.

Dad unplugged the microwave and poked inside the slow cooker. I shifted on my feet, feeling guilty. I'd forgotten about not overloading the outlet. Hmm, maybe I should conduct an experiment on what it takes to blow out a circuit. But Mom actually might kill me if I did.

The house phone rang. Startled, Dad and I exchanged confused looks.

Fact: Only 36 percent of US homes still have both landlines and cell phones. Mom refused to let go of our home phone because she was afraid of another hurricane disaster, like Jeanne and Frances, which had both hit Florida in September 2004. There'd been no electricity for over a week! Imagine: no AC, no TV, and NO INTERNET FOR TEN DAYS. Thankfully, that'd happened two years and one month before I was born.

The phone rang again. Dad answered the corded phone receiver.

"Hello?" He paused, nodding his head. "Sorry, Thomas, but Mira can't talk right now. She should be cleaning her room."

My shoulders fell.

"You too. Tell your parents I said hello."

"Sorry, Dad," I said after he hung up.

He ruffled my curls and with a tired smile said, "It's all good."

I decided I'd better get out of there before he changed his mind and grounded me. So I scooped my cell from the floor and plodded off.

Inside my room I pulled out my phone to text Thomas and apologize for cutting us off. I gasped. A shattered screen stared back at me. I pressed the power button. Nothing. I held the button in longer. The screen remained black. I pushed it over and over, but it was useless.

Superheated energy bounced around in my body at 291,000 miles per hour, like a star hurtling in space. Or like the grape plasma balls in the microwave. My head dizzy, I clutched the edge of my dresser.

I opened my mouth to scream, but the only sound that escaped was a nervous squeak.

I wanted to rush down the hall and beg Dad to take me to the store this very second to get a new cell. Or at least persuade him to let me use the family laptop so I could do an internet search on how to fix a broken iPhone. But I hesitated.

With Dad's days spent job hunting, his patience was wearing thin. And after my plasma ball experiment had gone wrong, I didn't want to push my luck. Maybe it'd be better to wait for Mom to get home from work.

I hated that Dad was so miserable since he'd lost his job. I hated that my experiment had caused a power outage. But I really, *really* hated that my phone was dead.

"I live in a world of suck," I announced to no one.

Well, technically there was an audience of one. Sprawled across my bed, Sir Fig Newton paused his afternoon tongue bath. His paw hung in midair, and his lime-green eyes were wide, piercing into my thoughts.

"You get it, don't you, Fig?"

Fig blinked, an obvious nod to my situation, and resumed grooming his belly with steady determination.

My finger dragged across the phone's screen, tracing the spiderweb-shaped cracks. I'd only had it for two weeks. At the start of sixth grade, my parents had promised me a tablet if I made the honor roll all year. When I'd presented my final report card boasting straight As, I'd gotten Mom's hand-me-down iPhone instead.

I set it facedown on my dresser. Now I had nothing.

Thomas was gone. And just like that I had no way to reach him.

2

OUT-OF-THIS-WORLD AWESOME

It was strange not being able to reach Thomas. We'd been best friends since forever. Our dads had worked together at this large company called Harris that helps make defense and space technology. Really cool stuff like panoramic night-vision goggles and an ultra-powerful telescope that will find the universe's first stars and galaxies!

When our dads had discovered we lived on the same street, our moms had thought it would be fun to have a playdate. I don't exactly remember it, but all the embarrassing pictures on Mom's phone was evidence enough.

Every time Mom introduced the two of us to adults, she'd always gush about how adorable we were together the first time we met. Supposedly Thomas had wanted to color, but I'd insisted that we launch my new rocket instead. Who wouldn't want to watch the foam missile soar a hundred feet into the sky, simply from the power of my stomp and a blast of air?

Even worse was when Mom said how cute it would be if the two of us ended up dating. Dad would always add, "Yeah, when my baby girl's twenty-two." Gross!

Even with the miles between us, I was confident Thomas and I would stay best friends forever. That's what he said the day he left for DC, right after we promised to text every day and video-chat every week. My parents had to replace the broken phone, that's all. And the best time to let them know would be *after* a cleaned room.

Fueled by the need to get on my parents' good side, I pinched my thumb and forefinger around my Muppets Beaker and Dr. Bunsen sock and rescued it from a smothering pile of *Science World* magazines, safety goggles, and a kitchen timer. I held the sock up to my nose and sniffed. There was a stink, kind of like burnt toast, though nowhere near sweaty-armpit territory. I tossed the sock onto the fold-and-put-away pile and fished out another, this one blue and covered in cat hair.

Fig licked the same belly spot over and over until his gray fur shined. In fact, Fig was picky about the cleanliness of everything. He even refused to use the litter box if it wasn't scooped after every, um, bathroom break. I'd timed his bathing session once, to maintain the sanctity of indisputable facts, and clocked an entire five minutes of him picking away claw jam with his teeth. Too bad I couldn't train Fig to clean my room.

I shook my favorite shirt, causing kitty litter and potato chip crumbs to shoot off in multiple directions. A gift from Thomas, it was licorice-red with a white cartoon drawing of Albert Einstein on the front, and the quote IMAGINATION IS MORE IMPORTANT THAN KNOWLEDGE across the back.

Clutching the shirt, my gaze roamed past my phone and settled on the lone picture on the dresser. The photo was from this past February, of my parents, Thomas, and me, with Fig snuggled in my arms, huddled in front of the space shuttle *Atlantis*. Fig hadn't really been there. Thomas had photoshopped him in as a joke to see if I'd notice. All it had taken for me was one glance, or 1.28 seconds. It had taken Mom and Dad almost half a minute.

Dressed in pressed khakis and a crisp, blue button-down, Dad towered over Mom's petite frame. Clean-shaven and rocking a short-cropped 'fro, he smiled from ear to ear. And Mom, her fiery-red hair blended into her short, long-sleeved dress emblazoned with the gold Starfleet logo on the chest. Thomas had pointed out how appropriate her Lieutenant Uhura costume was for spending the day at the Kennedy Space Center.

"Did you know that the original *Star Trek* actress was a for-reals astronaut recruiter?" he'd asked. "She not only recruited the first Black American to be launched into space, Guion Bluford Jr., but also Sally Ride, the first female American astronaut."

I'd elbowed his chest, a warning not to encourage my mom's obsession for embarrassing costumes.

For a future astronomer *and* astronaut like myself, that day had been out-of-this-world awesome. We'd toured historic launch sites and working spaceflight facilities,

13

strapped in for an eight-and-a-half-minute simulated space shuttle ascent into orbit, and met astronaut Fred Gregory. He'd been the first Black American to pilot a shuttle mission, all the way back in 1985!

"Who here wants to be an astronaut when they grow up?" Mr. Gregory had asked the small crowd gathered in front of him. Almost every kid's hand had shot into the air, including mine. Mr. Gregory had chuckled at my arm waving wildly about. "Looks like someone here is *really* excited about space."

I'd nodded vigorously. "I'm going to be the first person to walk on Mars."

"Ah yes, the Red Planet," Mr. Gregory said. "Half the size of Earth, it's a dusty, cold desert world that takes eight months for a spaceship to get to. NASA believes that the first Mars landing with a crew could happen sometime in the 2030s.

"If you believe it and work hard for it, then anything is possible," he said with a big smile and a wink.

The next room we visited was the US Astronaut Hall of Fame, where I gawked at the portraits of space heroes and legends. Of the ninety-seven faces staring back, only nine were women. Thomas and I stopped in front of Dr. Ellen Ochoa's plaque. Inducted in 2017, she was the world's first Latina astronaut. Thomas hit the "more info" button on our handheld digital tour guide and read aloud.

"Dr. Ellen Ochoa, a classical flutist for twenty-five years, brought her flute with her onto the space shuttle. She had to strap down her feet so she wouldn't float and spin around while she played.

"Ha! Maybe you can bring a basketball with you on your first mission and make the first slam dunk in space."

Thomas snickered, but I stood there silently. After a few minutes of my eyes locked on the wall of astronauts, Thomas leaned in to me and said, "Your picture will be up there too someday, Miranium."

It was what I wanted more than anything else.

A month later both Thomas's dad and my dad were laid off, along with a whole bunch of other engineers at Harris. Mom blamed it on "cutbacks." Dad said it was because they'd lost some big contract with the military. Thomas's dad got a new job in DC. But no matter how many resumes Dad had sent, he still hadn't found another job.

I tossed my Einstein shirt onto the dresser, burying the photo.

I so wanted to tell Thomas about my busted cell phone, but I pushed play on my old iPod instead. Pharrell Williams belted out instructions to clap along if you felt happy.

I strutted around the room, my head sliding from side to side as I continued to pick through the pile on the floor. Fig shared my love of music. Still busy primping, his white-tipped tail twitched along with the beat. I grabbed Fig's front paws and waved them back and forth. If only I could make Dad this happy.

I froze. "That's it, Fig."

Our eyes locked, and he released a sharp "maow" as he wriggled free.

"If anything can help me make Dad happy again," I said, my voice growing bubbly, "it's science."

101 FACIAL EXPRESSIONS

Could music really save Dad from his funk?

Sure, at the first sight of my phone's shattered screen, my heart had splintered into a million pieces. But then some "Happy" music had helped dilute the pain. This could work.

I sat at my desk surrounded by a pile of books, including *101 Kids' Super Fun Science Experiments* and *Get the Inside (and Outside!) Scoop on the Human Body*, and spent most of the afternoon conducting background research on music.

The facts: Our heartbeat falls into sync with a song's rhythm. A slow heart rate tells our brain that something sad is happening. A rapid pulse equals excitement. A dreamy rhythm can mean love or joy. Tone is just as important. A "major key" music piece communicates cheer, while a "minor key" mirrors grief.

My hypothesis? With the right music Dad's mood could escape his black hole and shine bright again like the aurora borealis.

Prying him away from his job hunt wouldn't be easy, so I couldn't waste what would probably be only one opportunity to help him. Experiments need at least twenty test subjects to ensure reliable data. But in this case, I'd be happy if I could get just one before fixing Dad.

I was already down three guaranteed subjects, with Thomas and his parents in DC. And Gran Williams was way too far away to get to on my bike.

Sir Fig Newton head-butted my ankle, aware of my fading excitement. I scratched under his chin. He leaned in, his eyes shut in bliss. I bent down and kissed his snout. Although his sweet-smelling breath was an improvement over burped-tuna-flavored funk, my nose still wrinkled.

Fig always made a great test subject and an awesome assistant. He had the same four qualities as any great scientist: he was patient, curious, observant, and persistent. But I wouldn't be keeping within my experiment's controlled variables if I used a nonhuman participant.

There *was* my neighbor and fellow space lover, Mrs. Branson. She would be the perfect test subject. After having her baby, Sabrina, Mrs. B always looked like she'd just crawled out of bed. Who better to test for mood changes?

The doorbell rang down the hall, halting my momentum on saving my dad.

"Mira!" Dad's voice called tiredly. "Get the door."

I jumped out of my chair. Fig mirrored my lead, snaking in and out of my stride.

The doorbell chimed again. This time with bothersome three-in-a-row buzzes.

My hand froze a nanosecond before turning the lock. Stretched onto my tippy toes, I peeked through the peephole. My breath sucked in at the full-figure, fish-eye view: hands shoved into her jean skirt pockets; a natural big poof of kinky curls like a massive, beautiful star cluster framing her face; and that silly fake white flower tucked behind her right ear.

Tamika Smith. My nemesis.

Sir Fig Newton crouched low, his ears flattened.

"I can hear you." Tamika's muffled voice seeped through the front door.

I backed away and fled to the family room. Fig scampered at my heels. Dad sat hunched over in his recliner, his weary gaze glued to the computer in his lap.

The doorbell struck again. The three shrill notes of someone demanding to be let in.

Fact: According to my research, people have twenty-one expressions, all a smashed-up combination of six: sadness, happiness, fear, anger, disgust, and surprise. Cats, however, have a minimum of 101 facial expressions. No big surprise that cats are far superior beings. Dads are simpler. Mine was moving into irritated territory, his chair squeaking.

"Didn't I ask you to get that?"

"It's this annoying girl from school. Can you get rid of her for me? Please?"

Dad shut the laptop and sat up. Fig pawed at Dad's

ashy knees. "You know, Mira, you're old enough now to face your own battles."

I clasped my hands together in front of my chest. "I know, but Tamika is a super pest. Just tell her . . . tell her I'm sick. Pretty please? With sprinkles and gummy bears on top?"

Tamika was one of those students that every teacher adored and that annoyed her classmates. I supposed she must have been sniffing around, wanting to get a whiff of my science project for next year. She might have won first place the last four years, but my runner-up status was nothing to sneeze at. I was her only real competition. Even though the science fair was over six months away, my declaration "I'll be number one next year!" at the last awards ceremony must have really gotten to her. Why else would she be here?

"Mira," Dad warned.

"Fine."

I trudged to the front door. Fig slunk by my side. I reluctantly opened the door.

"Hi, *El*mira."

Tamika's voice scratched my nerves. She was the only

person in the Milky Way who called me by my full name, extra emphasis on the first syllable. Even my namesake, Gran, used my preferred alias. Fig echoed my thoughts with a snarling hiss.

Before Tamika could say another word, I covered my mouth and burst into a coughing attack.

One of her thick eyebrows shot up. "Are you sick?"

"Yeeeaaah." I dragged out my response with a raspy voice.

"My mom's chicken noodle soup is the perfect antidote." She leaned against the doorway. "You probably don't know this, but it's not just granny folklore. One published study shows that the soup inhibits the movement of neutrophils, the most common type of white blood cell that defends against infection."

Tamika stood there with a smug grin. My face wore a dull stare.

"Oh, maybe I should explain," she said, straightening the oversized flower behind her ear. "By inhibiting the migration of these infection-fighting cells, chicken soup helps reduce upper-respiratory cold symptoms. There's other evidence that chicken soup improves the function of cilia. Not to be confused with nasal hair, cilia are microscopic hairlike strands farther back in the nose that move mucus out of the sinuses."

Tamika pointed at her nose, slowly sounding out the word—"SIH-lee-uh"—as if she were onstage for a spelling bee. I *knew* what cilia were. Fig's tail thrashed back and forth. I rubbed my nose and faked another cough.

"My mom's recipe is guaranteed to drain any stuffy sinuses. Her secret ingredient is one drop of CaJohn's Lethal Ingestion," Tamika said, rocking in her sneakers. "It's the world's hottest hot sauce without any extracts. It has over one million Scoville units!"

"Thanks, but I don't like spicy."

I started to close the door. Tamika stepped closer, thwarting my escape. I frowned. What did I have to do to get her off my front porch?

"Well, make sure to wash your hands with antibacterial soap." She rubbed her hands together, as if I needed a lesson on hygiene. "You don't want to miss STEM Girls camp. It starts in precisely thirteen days!"

I held back an eye roll. Of *course* I wouldn't miss STEM Girls. It was the best summer camp. For five days, girls in fourth grade through seventh grade from all over Brevard County learned all kinds of neat stuff about science, technology, engineering, and mathematics. I'd been faithfully going since fourth grade. Unfortunately, so had Tamika.

"Remember my experiment?" she continued. "Antibacterial soap growing the lowest number of bacterial colonies, compared to regular soap, hand sanitizer, and a plain-water rinse? It took first place in third grade."

I scowled. So it *was* the science fair that had brought Tamika to my doorstep, as hypothesized. Did she really need to rub in her first-place reign? Fig seemed to sense my exasperation and planted his chonky body between me and my nemesis.

"Well, bed rest is what the doctor ordered," I croaked.

Tamika shrugged, her face finally registering defeat. "Feel better."

I nodded as I closed the front door. Once the lock clicked, I scratched my guard kitty under his chin. "Nice teamwork, Sir Fig Newton. We beat the enemy."

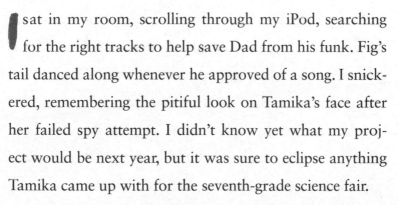

THE GREATEST SCIENTIST

I sat in my room, scrolling through my iPod, searching for the right tracks to help save Dad from his funk. Fig's tail danced along whenever he approved of a song. I snickered, remembering the pitiful look on Tamika's face after her failed spy attempt. I didn't know yet what my project would be next year, but it was sure to eclipse anything Tamika came up with for the seventh-grade science fair.

I was almost done with the perfect playlist when my bedroom door flew open, sending Fig scurrying across the room. Mom might have been petite, but her body still had a habit of looming in the doorway. My back snapped to attention.

Mom's eyes grazed over the unmade bed, piles of clothes, and cluttered desk. Her freckled nose scrunched in disgust at the litter scattered in front of Fig's bathroom box. Her mood was ablaze like her red hair.

"It appears somebody slacked off today." Mom crossed her arms.

Uh-oh. At the beginning of the year, I'd made the mistake of swearing on my life, with one hand over my heart and the other on Mom's treasured bible, *Housekeeping 101: Tips to the Perfect Home*, that "I, Mira Williams, will keep a spotless bedroom in exchange for a generous allowance." I'd been so caught up in saving Dad, I'd forgotten about my promise. My room still looked as if a Category 5 hurricane had hit.

I leapt from my desk and started to shove random objects into their appropriate homes, hoping Mom would appreciate the effort. A handful of markers into my WORLD'S GREATEST SCIENTIST cup. A red sneaker next to its mate on the shoe rack in my closet.

"Halt!"

I froze.

"You know the rules. This should have all been done before lunch."

My head drooped.

"As per our agreement," Mom barked, "anytime you fail to meet your obligations, there will be consequences."

"But—but if a messy desk is a sign of a messy mind, then imagine what an empty desk means!"

"Quoting Einstein is not getting you out of this one." Mom slipped off her suit jacket and twisted it with a kung fu grip. "Tonight, young lady, you're on dish duty."

Ugh, dishes! The only disaster worse than my room was the kitchen after Dad attempted to cook. I kicked at the not-so-smelly clothes pile.

Mom's harsh gaze softened. "Mira, honey, sometimes we have to do things we don't like." She smoothed out the wrinkles in her not-at-all-like-Mom blouse and gray skirt.

I was still annoyed, but I nodded. Dad wasn't the only miserable one since he'd lost his job. Mom had stopped volunteering with the community theater and started working at an accounting office. Now she spent all day "crunching numbers."

I liked to imagine that Mom's job was to inhale bags of crunchy potato chips and document how many chips were really inside. No matter how big the bag, why was over half of it always stale air?

Fact: Companies pump the bag with nitrogen gas to prevent the chips from becoming potato crumbs, proven by my experiment in the third grade. How *that* had lost against what type of soap kills the most germs, I'll never understand.

"Crunching numbers," however, wasn't as fun as it sounded. Mom managed other people's money, doing complicated calculations to figure out how much they owed the government.

"Dinner's ready!" Dad hollered.

Mom and I exchanged worried glances. The only mess worse than the damage made in the kitchen was the so-called food Dad served us. Despite my many protests of a weak stomach, Mom argued that we couldn't afford takeout and insisted we tough it out.

"Time to face the dinner plate," Mom murmured, grimacing as the smell of burnt beef and sour tomato sauce filled the room.

"Wait." From the top of my second-place science

fair trophy, I snatched my plastic fangs from last year's Halloween costume. I held the fake teeth out to Mom and nodded at her dark and drab suit. "To finish off your look."

Her forehead wrinkled.

I waved the plastic fangs. "Because doing stuff you don't like sucks."

A grin crept across Mom's face. She released the grip on her jacket and took the fake teeth. "C'mon, dinnertime."

"Be there in ten minutes."

"Make it five."

"Yes, ma'am." I saluted at her back as she left the room.

I picked up my dead phone from the dresser and slipped it into my back pocket. Once my parents were full and relaxed after dinner, I would tell them about my dire situation. I'd lost some points with my messy room, but I was sure they'd understand the need for a new phone.

I removed the Einstein shirt covering my favorite photo. All the people I loved most stared back at me: Thomas, Sir Fig Newton, Dad, and Mom in her *Star Trek* outfit. It was the last time Mom had dressed up.

Before she'd started crunching numbers, it had been

normal for Mom to shop at the grocery store in a Mary Poppins costume, or to drop me off at school wrapped in a white dress, wearing a brown wig with a bun on each side of her head. Though, it got less cool having Princess Leia drop me off as I got older.

Mom said that the only way to find out who you really were was by trying on something new. Maybe that's why she loved dressing up in her embarrassing costumes. Or maybe not. I wasn't quite sure why Mom still had no clue about herself. I knew exactly who *I* was.

I knew, for instance, that I was going to be an astronomer and one day walk on Mars and maybe even live on the next International Space Station. People would call me Dr. Mira Williams, like Dr. Sally Ride. Not like a medical doctor, but an astrophysicist—a scientist who studies the planets, stars, and other objects in space and how they work. And someday the world would refer to me as the greatest scientist who'd ever lived. After Einstein, of course.

Maybe I would earn the title after I determined if I'd been born allergic to cleaning or if the aversion had been learned. Or once I figured out how to travel faster than the speed of light. Not only would that come in handy for my first NASA mission, but then I could also meet up with Thomas in DC on the same day he'd moved. Maybe even prevent our dads from getting fired in the first place.

Fig dropped off my bed and padded across the floor. Even at his size he easily leapt onto the dresser. He pawed at the picture frame and began to purr.

"You're right, Fig. Mom and Dad used to be happy."

However, it was like a ginormous star had exploded when Dad lost his job. A black hole had been born. The heaviness hanging over our family was enormous, and my parents were stuck at the event horizon. If they crossed it, they'd fall into the void and never escape. Some scientists believe they'd burn up. Some think they'd be *spaghettified*— stretched thin until they were ripped in two.

Since I was at a safe distance from their troubles, I'd never see them fall in. My parents would appear frozen at the hole's edge. And slowly, eventually, their image would fade away.

My Save Dad from His Funk project was sure to bring back his gut-busting laughs. I could even make a playlist for Mom. It would work. It had to work. I refused to let my parents get sucked into the void.

5

STATE OF EMERGENCY

I joined Mom and Dad at the dining room table, the second hand of the wall clock chiming in with their conversation. Fig gathered in a tight ball at my bare feet. I shoveled stale-smelling chili onto my plate and poked my fork at the lumpy chunks of beef, kidney beans, and vegetables. Even a heavy dose of Tamika's hot sauce wouldn't be able to bury the bitter aftertaste.

"The funniest thing happened at work today," Mom said.

Dad passed her the salad and raised his eyebrows. "I

don't think I've ever heard you use the words 'funny' and 'work' in the same sentence."

Mom playfully snatched the bowl and scooped a healthy serving. "A client asked if he could claim his dog as a dependent on his tax return. I kindly explained that he couldn't, but he proceeded to argue that it costs as much to keep Buster as it does himself."

"You hear that, Fig Newton?" Dad chuckled. "Sounds like you need to pull your own weight around here."

I nudged Fig with my big toe. He gave a slight stir but remained curled on the floor.

Mom babbled on about some new tax law and unhappy clients, with Dad nodding along. My busted cell phone lay at rest in my lap. My fingers grazed the shattered glass. Releasing a heavy sigh, I slathered butter all over a piece of warm corn bread. Dry bits crumbled onto my plate.

"So," Mom said, "how's the job search coming along?"

Dad's face was pained. Mom drowned her salad in ranch dressing. With every bite the crunch of lettuce disturbed the uncomfortable silence. Not once did she take her eyes off Dad. Suddenly he rose from his chair.

"How about some tea?" His voice was calm, yet barely audible.

Without waiting for a response, he marched to the kitchen.

Mom pushed away her plate, her mood not improved.

"Since you clearly weren't cleaning your room, what did *you* do all day?"

My hand darted again toward the phone in my lap. Maybe this time the screen would be intact. Nope. Somehow the cracks seemed wider.

"Mira?" Mom's voice softened.

Before I could answer, Dad strode back into the dining room, his face still weary but less upset. He set a steaming mug in front of Mom, rested his empty hand on her shoulder, and kissed the top of her head. She gave a small smile as he settled back in his chair with his own cup. With the tension cracked, I knew I had to seize the moment.

"We have a state of emergency."

Both my parents' heads swung in my direction. I set the iPhone on the table.

"I need a new phone."

"What! What happened? I just gave you this." Frowning,

Mom picked it up, scrutinizing every inch. Light from the overhead fixture bounced off the shattered screen. Specks jerked across the wall. Fig chittered, his head bouncing from side to side, following the dancing dots.

I winced, seeing Mom's disappointed expression. "It wasn't my fault, I swear."

I explained that the phone had accidentally dropped onto the kitchen floor while I'd been talking to Thomas, but left out the part about the exploding grapes causing a power outage. I didn't want to give Mom more reason to scold me.

Her scowl deepened as she handed the phone over to Dad. "I'm sorry, Mira, but you know we can't afford to replace this right now."

Agony seared across my chest. "But how will Thomas and I keep in touch?"

"He can call you on the landline," Mom said.

"And there's always email," Dad added, setting the cracked screen facedown on the table.

"But *you're* always on the laptop."

Sadness shadowed Dad's face again.

"Once you've finished cleaning your room for the

day," Mom intervened, "then Dad will give you an hour or two on the family computer. Right?" She gave him a meaningful glance. He hesitated and then nodded, though it looked reluctant.

My body stiffened. I stared at my broken phone, lips pressed together to prevent an angry tirade. This was *not* supposed to turn out like this. First no tablet. Now no phone. I was no longer at a safe distance, staring at my frozen parents at the black hole's edge. I was stuck with them at the event horizon.

Something heavy pounced onto my chest as I slept, and my exhale whistled like Gran's teakettle. A blast of sweet, hot breath tickled my nose, followed by a furry smack against my cheek.

"Why does your breath still smell weird?" my voice croaked.

A high-pitched "maow" vibrated in my ears. My eyes fluttered open and zeroed in on the glowing green digits of my alarm clock. 5:42. I'd been in the middle of dreaming that I'd won the title of All-Time Greatest Scientist after discovering the first wormhole.

This discovery supported Einstein's idea that the universe could be bent back on itself. One end of the wormhole was at my house, and the other end was at Mars. Once I jumped through it, I'd end up on the Red Planet in the blink of an eye. Tamika had been handing me the award—a big scowl on her face—right when I'd been rudely awoken.

I turned to face Fig and ruffled his gray fur. "You'd better not have gotten into something you shouldn't have. Chocolate can be lethal for cats, you know."

I rested my hand on Fig's left side, just behind his front leg, checking for an abnormal heart rhythm. "Pulse is normal. No tremors and no seizures, so I guess you're okay."

I slithered out of bed. You'd think I'd be used to this horrific hour since Fig greeted me at the same time, give or take twenty minutes, every morning. But I wasn't a fan of waking up against my will. I couldn't even get excited about emailing Thomas today, since that wouldn't happen until after I cleaned my room.

My feet dragged like a sleepwalking zombie's across the plush carpet over to Fig's bathroom. Thanks to his fascination with plastic, something I discovered when the shower curtain was riddled with tiny bite marks, my bedroom now had the honor of housing his litter box.

Even in my drowsy state, my brain puzzled over the increase in, um, number one clumps. For the third day in a row. How could Fig's teeny bladder produce so much liquid?

I carried a full scoop of litter—not once but twice—down the hall to the bathroom and dumped it into the toilet. Fig wound in and out of my stride, with an occasional meow reminder of the more pertinent matter at hand. Breakfast.

My eyes, barely slits, cringed against the harsh overhead light glowing above the stove. Fig's head bumped against my leg in unison with his repetitive, "Maow. Maow. Maow." Translation: *Food. Food. Food.*

My hands felt for the cupboard door and lugged out the supersized bag of cat food. Fat bold letters promised A NEW AND IMPROVED FLAVOR. How could they know this? Had a bunch of cats sat around a boardroom table raising their paws? Or had some poor guy had to endure a taste test? Yuck.

Dry bits clinked into Fig's bowl on the counter. His

front paws stretched like a slinky as he leaned against the cupboard, paws inches from the countertop. He dropped back down, and his nails clicked against the linoleum as he followed me into the eat-in area. My big toe smacked against something—hard—and Fig's water bowl slid across the floor.

"Mother Marie Curie." I grimaced, my senses now fully awake.

Yet the floor and the bowl were bone-dry. I left the empty water bowl in its new location and placed his food dish on the feeding mat.

Sir Fig Newton charged at his breakfast. I figured that, like every other morning, he would inhale the entire bowl in thirty seconds flat—the one thing in this world he did with speed and precision—followed by a frozen pause and a low, rumbling "Urp."

But this morning was different.

Fig nibbled on the dry food. The crunching stopped as his nose pushed around the large portion of remaining bits. After a few more bites, Fig trotted out of the kitchen. I frowned. Something wasn't right. I followed him back to my bedroom, and held my breath as he settled onto my bed for his midmorning nap.

Maybe he'd had so much water that his tummy only had enough room for a teaspoon of food? With the scorching summer heat, who could blame the poor guy?

I opened the blinds, exposing the rising sun. Fig flipped onto his back and stretched his front legs long, toes spread wide. A sunbeam spotlighted the rise and fall of his white belly.

I released a heavy sigh and switched my focus to cleaning my room. I picked through the clothes scattered on the carpet, silently repeating Dad's favorite phrase, *It's all good*. My stomach gurgled in disagreement.

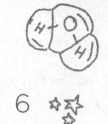

6

THE MAD SCIENTIST

Dad towered in my bedroom doorway, the family laptop in hand.

"This room needs to be spotless before you can email Thomas," he commanded.

"I know, I know. It already is." I put both hands behind my back and crossed my fingers.

Dad's head turned from shoulder to shoulder like the ticking second hand of the clock in the dining room. His gaze rolled over my desk, cleared of any books or magazines. Both my dresser and bookshelf were dust-free.

Nothing littered the floor, not even one dirty sock. His stare hesitated on a glass measuring cup hiding behind my alarm clock on the nightstand.

Oh no! How'd I missed that? The cup was half-filled with a bluish substance from a project started before summer, testing whether people's perceptions of taste were influenced by their sight.

"Foreign substances." Dad typed away on the laptop, balancing it in his left hand while pecking away with his right. "Unmade bed—"

"But Sir Fig Newton's using it!"

Fig lifted his head, yawned, and promptly went back to his nap. I grinned. The mammoth of fur always had my back.

"Unmade bed," Dad repeated, banging on the keyboard again.

I slumped onto the edge of my bed and gave a big sigh. "I guess I'll never talk to Thomas again."

Dad snapped the computer shut and sat next to me. He picked at his frazzled 'fro, gloom coloring his face. "I know things have been hard, Mira, since I lost my job. I'm sorry we can't replace the phone, but I promise that as soon as

I'm working again, everything will go back to normal."

"When will that be?"

Dad shrugged. "As long as it takes."

"But it's already been *forever*."

He rested a hand on my shoulder. Although his touch was light, the heaviness in his brown eyes weighed us both down.

Suddenly a grin snuck across Dad's face. I raised my eyebrows in surprise.

"Let's make a deal," he said. "How about you promise to finish cleaning your room before your mother gets home, and I'll let you use the laptop right now."

I gasped. "I promise!" I jumped off the bed and marked a large X across my chest. Dad stood up, holding out the computer. Instead of taking it, I wrapped my arms tight around his wiry frame. "Thanks, Dad."

"It really is all good, Mira girl," he said, ruffling my curls. He placed the laptop into my open palms and left the room, whistling an upbeat tune.

Itching to finally catch up with Thomas, I dashed to my desk and logged in to my email account. My eyes fixed on the screen: three unread messages. I opened the first one.

From: Thomas Thompson

To: Mira Williams

Date: Jun 18, 10:38 AM

Subject: What happened?

Hey, Miranium. One moment I'm watching flaming grapes, the next, I'm in the dark. What happened? I tried calling you back, but it kept going to voicemail, so I tried the house phone, but your dad said you're cleaning your room. Cleaning your room??? Did you hit your head when the grapes exploded?

I'll just be sitting here saving the world or maybe even the universe on my PlayStation.

Call me back!

Thomas

Hitting my head would've been a billion times better than dropping my phone. Then my life wouldn't have been so messed up. I sped on to the next two emails.

From: Thomas Thompson

To: Mira Williams

Date: Jun 18, 5:15 PM

Subject: RE: What happened?

OK, I'm worried. Maybe you really did hit your head and you have a concussion and you don't remember who I am. It's the only logical explanation for why you haven't called me back! Or sent an email or a text or messaged via a pigeon.

Did you know that the US Army Signal Corps used 600 pigeons during WWI?!

Where are you?

Write me back!

Thomas

From: Thomas Thompson

To: Mira Williams

Date: Jun 19, 8:38 AM

Subject: RE: What happened?

Are you still alive?

Unaware of my plight, poor Thomas was obviously bothered by my unusual silence. I quickly hit reply. My fingers raced across the keyboard. I was typing so fast, I barely saw what I was writing. I didn't even pause to read my response before clicking send.

From: Mira Williams

To: Thomas Thompson

Date: Jun 19, 10:02 AM

Subject: RE: What happened?

Hi Thomas. Im still alive, but my life is over. My cell phon is dead. I repeat: MY. PHONE. IS. DEAD.

And even worse, my parents cant replace it right now. So you have to call me on the house phone for our weekly chats and email instead of text. With my dad on the laptop 24/7 lookin for jobs, I'll only be able to get on the computer an hour or so a day, but none of that really matters, cause once my dad gets a job, everything will go back to normal.

I'm starting a new experiment. A mood-music

project to help my dad out of his funk. I'll be
testing it out on my neighbor Mrs B today while
your saving the world or universe or whatever.

Best friendz forever!

Mira

Now that Thomas and I were back in contact, it was time to put my plan for Dad into action. I arrived in my neighbor's kitchen, my backpack slung over my shoulder, ready to test my theory that music could fix Dad's mood. Despite the sleeping bags under her eyes, Mrs. Branson made lively "ooh" and "aah" faces at her daughter, Sabrina, while waving a purple rattle. Sitting in a lion baby seat at Mrs. B's sock-covered feet, Sabrina stared with intense fascination.

Mrs. and Mr. Branson had moved in next door a little over a year ago. The millisecond I'd found out that Mrs. B was an aerospace engineer at NASA, I'd known we would be friends. For hours I'd listened to her tell stories about designing and testing spacecrafts and satellites. We'd even spent a weekend building a LEGO space station. She'd told me all about the new Mars rover launching next year, and how she'd worked on the team to help make sure it'll land safely!

Mrs. B always encouraged my love of astronomy, not at all joking whenever she laughed and said, "One day you'll fly your first mission in one of the shuttles I worked on. Won't that be a hoot?" But after Sabrina had been born a few months ago, our space talks had always been cut short.

Her kitchen reminded me of ours last night before I'd washed a mountain of dinner dishes. Empty baby bottles and opened boxes of mac 'n' cheese were surrounded by stuffed animals on the countertop. Dirty pots and pans cluttered the sink.

Mrs. B leaned over and tickled Sabrina's belly. Sabrina gurgled in return.

Instead of wearing a summer dress with her hair hugging her shoulders, my neighbor's hair was pulled into a messy bun, and yoga pants and a snug tee showed off her curvy figure. Before Sabrina, I'd never seen Mrs. B without straight hair. The first time I'd witnessed her black curls, I'd been shocked.

"You have curly hair. Just like me!"

"Yeah, I don't have time to blow it out. What's the point when this little one loves to grab everything she can get her tiny fingers around?" Mrs. B had laughed.

"It's pretty when it's straight," I'd said, "but I kind of like it better curly."

Now I thought about how hard it must be to clean a whole house, dress up, *and* cook dinner when taking care of a newborn that needed constant attention. While trying to have our usual space talk, it made me dizzy just watching Mrs. B feed, change, calm, and entertain Sabrina. All I had was a claw-picking fat cat napping on my bed, and I could barely keep my room clean.

"So, what experiment are you working on this time?" Mrs. B asked. "Another one on black holes? Or phases of the moon?"

"Nope, not this time," I replied. "I'm trying to prove that people can change their mood through music."

"I can attest to that, honey." Mrs. Branson nodded. "Whenever I hear 'Let's Stay Together,' I start bawling. Happy tears. That was my baby sister's first wedding dance."

After wiping the drool from Sabrina's face, Mrs. B put

the slobber monster down for a nap. We moved into the family room. I unzipped my backpack and removed a stopwatch, a notebook, a pen, and my iPod. Buzzing with excitement to test my hypothesis, I slipped the iPod into her speaker dock.

"I just need you to listen to some songs, tell me your mood, and let me take your resting heart rate."

I stood in front of Mrs. B, now propped on the edge of the sofa, my pen hovering over my notebook. "On a scale of one to ten, rate your current stress level."

"I miss my job, but I'll be going back soon without Sabrina by my side, and . . ." Mrs. Branson paused, her lips set in a grim line as if her thoughts were playing tug-of-war. "Definitely an eight."

I jotted down her response. "How would you rate your energy level?"

"Two."

"How would you describe your current mood?"

"Anxious." Her leg bounced repeatedly in agreement.

I placed my middle and pointer fingers on the inside of Mrs. B's left wrist and took her pulse using the stopwatch. I counted the beats, a total of fifty-five, for thirty seconds.

I scribbled *110 beats* next to the words "Initial Resting Heart Rate" in my notebook.

"Okay, as you listen to the music, pay attention to how you feel."

I scrolled through the playlists until I found the one labeled On-the-Go and pressed play. A saxophone softly hummed, and was soon joined by a flute and piano. Mrs. B's leg stopped bouncing. Her eyes closed as she melted back into the couch, humming along with the soothing tune. It sounded like that instrumental old-folks stuff played in doctor's office waiting rooms. Her expression, like Fig's satisfied calm while grooming, was definitely moving into happy territory.

After twenty seconds I hit pause and took Mrs. B's heart rate again. Down a full ten beats.

"What are your stress and energy levels now?" I asked.

"Five and . . . four."

"And your mood?"

"Better."

Grinning, I wiggled my brows. So far the results supported my hypothesis!

I forwarded to the next track and pressed play, and a

new song kicked on. A high-pitched howl wailed over frenetic guitar riffs, followed by booming drums. Eyes wide, Mrs. B lurched forward, her messy bun falling over to one side. Over the baby monitor Sabrina squealed, even louder than the lead singer. Without a word, but wearing a bitter look, Mrs. B pushed herself up onto her feet and stomped down the hall.

I dove for the docking station and in my rush accidentally smashed several of the buttons at the same time. I snatched the iPod from the speaker and stared in horror. The playlist was gone. In its place there were instructions on how to create an On-the-Go playlist.

Super. I still had my crown for Short-Circuit Scientist.

"Did the mad scientist with her scary music startle you?" Mrs. Branson's voice crackled over the baby monitor.

I cringed at the words "mad scientist."

"Mommy feels the same way."

I shoved the iPod into my backpack, peeved about the deleted playlist and Mrs. B's snarky comments. Since when was I a mad scientist?

Five minutes later Mrs. B returned, Sabrina cradled in her arm, sucking on a pacifier. "This brown-eyed girl is wide awake," Mrs. Branson said. "We'll have to continue this another time."

I tried offering an understanding smile, but my face probably looked like some mashed-up combo of anger-sadness-disgust.

"Tell your parents hello," she said, switching the wiggly Sabrina to the opposite arm. "How're they doing?"

I shrugged. "Dad keeps saying it's all good."

"And he's right, you know." Mrs. B gave a tired smile. "I always say, you've got to have faith. This job upset is a flash in time. If you just believe, it'll all work out in the end."

I nodded. I wanted to believe, but I wasn't sure I could. Testing my hypothesis that music could change one's mood hadn't even made round one before screeching to an unexpected demise. I left Mrs. B's house and decided to head to the place that always made me feel welcomed and loved. My home away from home. Light-years from the event horizon.

7

THE STRONGEST ELEMENT IN THE UNIVERSE

Fact: There's no place like Thomas's home.

I leaned against the oak tree across the street from my best friend's old house, my grip tight around the handlebars of my bike. My hands relaxed at my first sight of the bright red FOR SALE sign poking out of the uncut grass. Even though Thomas was one hundred thousand (and one) miles away, there was comfort in being greeted by that metal sign. Sort of like an atom of hope that the Thompson family could change their minds and return home to Florida. Even though nothing would come

54

between our BFF status, it couldn't hurt to wish everything back to normal.

I could almost hear Thomas shouting to his mom, "Going out with Mira!" before slamming the front door shut. We'd cannonball into his pool, and he'd drown me in silly jokes, or we'd argue over *Star Wars* versus *Star Trek* and end up watching *Doctor Who* instead.

My eyes traveled from the FOR SALE sign to the basketball hoop, naked without a net, looming over the driveway. I'd spent forever coaching Thomas, and even though he'd shot nothing but bricks, I'd always cheered him on. "No moping allowed!" I'd say again and again. "Winning means never giving up." And although he'd kept on sulking, he'd always keep trying.

My fingers rubbed against the coarse bark of the oak, broken up like burnt cornflakes. I smiled, thinking about all those times when we were little and dressed up like astronauts. We wore orange space suits that my mom had made from old curtains, and square space helmets we'd made from cardboard boxes. We'd huddle together in a shuttle constructed out of chairs and bedsheets, and in T minus ten we'd blast off into space, visit the moon, Mars, the asteroid belt and beyond.

"You know what?" Thomas had asked once.

"No, what?"

"I bet when you're a *real* astronaut, you're going to find Planet Nine and it'll be named 'Mira'! And you'll discover a new element there, which will be the toughest, strongest, most indestructible element ever—just like you! And they'll call it 'miranium.'"

"Yeah!" I'd giggled. "Just like Pluto and plutonium."

I gazed up at the old tree now, thinking about how it had stood tall through many a hurricane. Maybe in addition to carbon, oxygen, and hydrogen, it also had a little bit of miranium, the strongest element in the universe, because nothing ever knocked it down. The live oak was so big, I imagined you could see it from space. Maybe even Mae Jemison had seen this very tree as she'd orbited Earth 126 times in the space shuttle *Endeavour*.

Dad had watched the 1992 launch from his own backyard when he was a kid. Before my phone broke, I'd watched the blastoff footage online all the time to remind myself that I too was meant to be a scientist and someday walk in space.

It hadn't been easy for Mae. She had first applied for admission to NASA's astronaut training program in 1985, but the *Challenger* disaster had delayed the process. But she didn't give up. When she reapplied a year later, she was one of fifteen candidates chosen from about two thousand! Mae Jemison was the first Black woman to be admitted into the NASA astronaut training program, the first Black woman astronaut, *AND* the first Black woman in space.

So what if my playlist had disappeared into the void? So what if I'd had a minor "mad scientist" malfunction? It had only taken me a few hours to put the playlist together. I could make another one. This was just an insignificant point in time, like my parents stuck in their funk.

I hopped back onto my bike and pedaled home, excited to return to work. I'd make another playlist to test out on Mrs. B, this time with no heavy screech—

Both my thoughts and my bike skidded to a stop as I reached my driveway. There she was, standing on the front porch talking to my dad. My nemesis. Tamika Smith.

"*El*mira. Feeling better?" Tamika asked with that snotty attitude and her head held up so high, you could see up her nose. "I suppose a bike ride, instead of bed rest, could be the antidote to phlegm."

"Tamika brought you some soup," Dad said, raising the Tupperware bowl in his hands. "Isn't that nice?"

"Yeah, that's nice." Slipping off my helmet, I made a mental note to pour every last drop down the drain the second she left. Who knew what ulterior motives were hidden in the ingredients?

"You sound satisfactory." Tamika's face scrunched in confusion. "No coughing or stuffy nose."

I was itching to order her away from my home. "Must have been one of those twenty-four-hour things."

Dad gave me a look but luckily didn't call me out. What he said instead was so much worse. "Why don't you two go play in Mira's room?"

My eyes bugged, the better to transmit my raging mind stream. *What are you doing? Never, ever, ever invite the enemy onto your home turf.* But all Dad gave me in return was one of those *I'm sorry* face-shrug combinations.

"A prodigious idea," Tamika said brightly.

Repressing an eye roll, I plodded into the house with Tamika at my heels. I stomped down the hall and into my room, Tamika trailing in my perturbed wake. Sir Fig Newton lay curled in a ball on my bed. Paws twitching, Fig was entering kitty la-la land. Hopefully not a nightmare like my current situation. If he was being chased by a pack of gargantuan Saint Bernards or, even worse, discovering that tuna-flavored cat food has gone extinct, at least he would experience the deep-sleep terror for only six to seven minutes. Who knew how long I'd have to endure Tamika's presence?

I plopped down at my desk. My saliva would soon boil, since my fury was approaching the Armstrong limit.

"Why are you really here, Tamika?" My eyes narrowed.

"Just checking up on you," she said, straightening that awful colossal flower planted behind her right ear. My guard was up. There had to be plotting behind the concerned expression. "I heard that Thomas moved to DC."

"Yeah. You're probably wondering about my science project for next year."

She shook her head, her face brightening. "Any ideas yet?"

Her fingers rifled through the loose papers on my desk. I swatted at her hand. She was more annoying than a swarm of lovebugs.

"*I'll* be exploring Kepler's third law." She wiggled her brows with a smug grin.

When I didn't respond, she continued with one of her smarter-than-thou explanations.

"That's the relationship between orbital period and distance. Planets in their elliptical orbits move faster when they're closer to the sun and slower when they're farther away. That's why the speed that a planet travels at is always changing." She cocked her head so far to one side, it looked as if her fake flower were weighing her head down. "You?"

I shrugged.

I wasn't about to admit that her project sounded pretty neat. Anyway, some of us were too busy with more important things, like saving parents from a funk, to be thinking about the science fair. I folded my hands together on top of my desk and nodded toward my bedroom door, hoping Miss Smarty-Pants could take a hint.

"Thanks for the soup," I said.

"Nothing wrong with being out of ideas, you know. Your project Can Black Holes Really Freeze Time? was a decent attempt"—Tamika shrugged—"but we can't all win first place."

Ugh, why did Dad have to let Tamika in? I gave her my "laser eyes." I imagined her head expanding, blowing up like a balloon. Once it reached the size of Astronaut Snoopy dressed in a NASA space suit from the Macy's Thanksgiving Day Parade, I pictured Tamika and her big head floating right out of my room.

She must have caught my look, because her tone became flat. "Well, guess I'll see you at camp. Glad you feel better. Enjoy the soup minus the hot sauce." Tamika spun on her heel and left.

Scowling, I threw my pen in her direction. It bounced off the doorjamb.

I turned toward Fig for sympathy, but he remained in a tight ball on my bed. Wait. Was he still in the same spot? He must have slept through the whole awful ordeal with Tamika.

The more I thought about it, the more I was sure that Fig had slept all day, except for the 5:42 a.m. wake-up call. None of his usual in-between-catnap checkups on me and the waking world. It was almost dinnertime, and Fig hadn't even begged for lunch. Now *that* was unheard of. Something really was wrong.

Frowning, I leaned in close. His belly slowly rose and fell. I poked his immense furry flesh. No head raise, evil glare, or paw swat. He just grunted, remaining in his dead-to-the-world state. I drew back, my body numb with fear.

"Dad!" I ran out of my room. "Dad. Something's wrong with . . ."

I veered to a stop at the end of the hall and lingered just out of sight. Mom and Dad were slouched at the dining room table, talking in hushed tones. The air was stiff, like the time Fig had chewed up the laces of every pair of Dad's shoes. This couldn't be good. The only time they sat in the dining room without food was when something was wrong.

Mom's chipped nail tapped against her cup in an anxious beat. "I can't believe you spent over a thousand dollars."

My eyes grew wide.

Dad released a heavy exhale. "I can't help that the funeral is this weekend."

I gasped. The only person I'd ever known who had died was my grandma Millie.

We'd gotten the call in the middle of the night. She'd

been in a car accident and was in a coma. I was eight and had only met Grandma Millie a few times. My mind would always go blank whenever I tried to picture her, except for her thick, straight hair. Fiery red, against fair white skin, like Mom. The only reason I'd cried was because I'd never seen Mom shake so hard. She was usually like a live oak, tall and strong against hurricane-force winds.

Now Mom blew into her cup but didn't take a sip. Her voice sounded shaky. "I don't know how we're going to take care of everything."

Dad squeezed Mom's hand. There was a long silence as they just stared at each other. My nerves twisted tighter than my curls.

My gut craved to tell Mom and Dad about all the weird stuff happening to Sir Fig Newton: sweet-smelling breath, lots of number one clumps, and no eating. Although Fig was practically comatose, I remained frozen at the event horizon. The black hole's gravitational pull was bad enough. I didn't want to push my parents in.

I inhaled deeply and trudged into the dining room. Mom welcomed my presence with a grim smile.

"Mira, sweetie, please join us." She patted the chair next to hers. "We need to talk."

I sat down. My fingers fidgeted with the woven place mat.

"Dad's best friend, from when they were growing up, he passed away," she said gently.

Mom rambled on about the funeral and Dad flying across the country.

My attention turned to Dad. The wrinkles between his brows were pulling his frown farther down. I wasn't sad about his friend like he was. But then I thought about it more. I'd already lost Thomas to DC. But what if I'd lost Thomas *forever* forever? It would be like . . . like being sucked into a black hole and spaghettified.

"You'll be staying with Gran Williams until Monday." Mom's voice registered again. "I'll drop you off tomorrow before I head in to work."

"Till Monday?" Oh no. Not Gran Williams. I couldn't leave Fig alone for that long. "You couldn't come get me after work?"

"With upcoming deadlines, I'll be working all weekend and late nights," Mom said. "Plus, your grandmother is looking forward to spending some time with you."

"Can Fig come?" I asked desperately, but I already knew the answer.

"I'm sorry, Mira, but you know her cat doesn't like to mingle with others."

And that included humans. Gran's cat, Viper, made the cat Lucifer from the *Cinderella* movie look like an angel. Of course, Viper never let his wicked side show in front of Gran. She never tolerated anything less than perfection. "Cleanliness is next to godliness" was her favorite phrase.

"But don't worry," Mom continued, "I'll take good care of Fig while you're gone."

If only I could persuade Mom to swear on her life, with one hand over her heart and the other on her favorite book, *Housekeeping 101: Tips to the Perfect Home*, that she'd measure Fig's water bowl daily and note his litter box amounts and food intake. But she had enough going on. My face bleak, I nodded.

Four long days trapped with Gran and Viper, separated from my poor sick Fig. Could this summer get any worse?

8

THE INDISPUTABLE FACTS

I kicked my muddy sneakers off by Gran's front door. A symphony of voices harmonizing a cappella blasted throughout her house. The singing was so strong, you'd have sworn a church choir had assembled in the living room.

Even though she was seventy years old and only 5'2", Gran looked towering in the foyer. Her cat, Viper, hovered by her heels, his glowing eyes following my every move. At first glance Gran almost appeared bald. Her scalp bristled with tight gray curls trimmed close. Her green wrap dress hung loose on her slim frame. But Gran was a lot tougher than she looked. Everyone in her hood knew Gran as "Hardball." She constantly called out neighbors on overgrown grass, inappropriate paint colors, and too bright Christmas lights. She said Jesus wouldn't like them.

Gran's manicured nails lifted up my chin, and her deep brown eyes inspected my solemn face. "Just want to get a good look at you now, Miss Mira." Her voice cut sharp and deep. "Since you rarely grace me with your presence, even though I only live an hour away."

I flinched.

"Go unpack." She nodded toward the stairs, her gold hoop earrings waving along. "Then come back down and we'll catch up."

I took my time unpacking, until I felt like I couldn't delay it any longer, then joined Gran in the living room. The couch crackled as I tried to get comfortable. Sweaty thighs + Florida heat + plastic-wrapped furniture = no sense whatsoever.

My last visit had been over four months ago—for Gran's birthday in January—and the house had been as spotless then as it was now. Books lined the three shelves in descending height order, flanked by a gold-framed photo on either side. Five of the pictures showcased the prize-winning Maine coons she'd raised over the years, most way before I was born, all male and each named after an archangel. The sixth photo was a high school graduation picture of Dad, his Afro so big, it didn't fit in the frame.

Next to a neat stack of magazines, *Cat Fantastic* on top, fresh roses sat on the end table, their sweet smell losing against Lysol. Not a speck of dust could be detected by the naked eye. Gran would have a heart attack if she ever stepped foot into my bedroom.

Still glued to Gran's heels, Viper snoozed in a curled ball on the plush carpet. Gran's secret to no signs of feline life—no evidence of cat hair or litter—could earn her a fortune.

"How are you, Miss Mira?" Gran's folded hands cradled her crossed knees.

"Do you want the polite answer," I asked, "or the honest-to-God truth?"

"Only the truth shall set you free," she said sternly. One

thing you had to respect about Gran, she was up-front no-nonsense.

I put my chin in my hands. "This summer *sucks*."

A frown cut across Gran's taut face. "I don't tolerate that language in my house."

"Sorry, Gran."

Although her face remained tight, her frown vanished. "Go on."

"First," I said, holding up one finger, "my best friend, Thomas, moved a million and one miles away to DC."

"Was that the skinny white boy with the shaggy hair?"

I gave a quick nod with my pout.

"What a shame. Seemed like a nice young man."

My middle finger joined my pointer. "My cell phone died."

"You kids." Gran rolled her eyes. "I didn't grow up with a cell phone, and I survived."

I should've known I'd get no sympathy for that one. Gran was so old-school, she had a flip phone that rarely left her purse. She didn't even have a computer.

"And three," I concluded, "Sir Fig Newton is sick."

Gran's face softened. She leaned over and stroked

Viper's slick black fur. "What's wrong with the little guy?"

I shrugged. "I know he's sick, but, like, I don't know for a *fact* he's sick."

Gran nodded.

"Fig's my best furry friend, and I don't want to lose him, too."

Gran narrowed her gaze. "You're a scientist, right?"

"Yes, ma'am."

"Then how would you prove your theory that Sir Fig Newton is sick?"

I leaned back into the plastic-wrapped couch. Gran was right. Sure, Mom and Dad didn't need anything more to worry about. Not without proof. But as the world's greatest scientist, I could surely determine whether Fig was really sick.

"Only one way to prove my hypothesis," I declared. "With the indisputable facts."

9

CAT FANTASTIC COMBUSTION

My first instinct to prove that Fig was sick was to consult an expert. But when I called Gran's vet from the old beige landline phone, I was told that she was stuck in surgery all day. The receptionist promised to pass on my message, but I couldn't sit around waiting for a call. Instead I convinced Gran to drop me off at the library while she ran errands. I wasn't leaving that musty old building without irrefutable proof that Sir Fig Newton was off his game.

The automatic entrance doors slid open, and a blast

of cold air struck my face. The library's air conditioner whined against the summer heat streaming through the floor-to-ceiling windows. I strolled past a skinny dude reading a book in a worn leather chair, and a white-haired gang of old ladies inside one of those meeting rooms, their heated debate and clicking knitting needles seeping through the closed door.

The odds of finding kids my age here during the summer were as slim as the chance that Dad would whip up a delicious meal. I wondered how he was doing. Between only one job interview this summer and his childhood friend's funeral, I was afraid I'd never see him laugh again. I'd finished remaking my playlist before arriving at Gran's, but there hadn't been enough time to retest it.

Pushing away the pangs of guilt, I approached the librarian at the welcome desk. Fig needed my help right now.

"What can I do for you today?" she asked, her cheeks rosy as if she'd just escaped a tickle attack. I squinted, blinded by her carnation-colored suit.

"My cat's sick and I need to figure out what's wrong."

"Sorry about your cat." Tickled Pink offered a somber

smile. "We have an extensive nonfiction section, which is sure to cover all kinds of cat health issues."

My favorite teacher, Miss Kirker, always stressed that when conducting research, we should use various sources, both on- and off-line. She'd shake her head in that grown-up way whenever students relied only on online search engines and online encyclopedias. Unfortunately, Gran was picking me up in less than two hours.

"I don't have that kind of time, sorry. Where can I get on the internet?"

"Wait, didn't I help you find books on science experiments a while back?" She pushed up her cotton-candy-pink glasses. "Something to do with space?"

I nodded, furrowing my brow. "On black holes. But that was in January."

"I'm good with faces." She grinned.

Had she had a different favorite color the last time I was here? I probably would've remembered a librarian drowned in pink.

"Come with me."

I followed Tickled Pink and her sweet rose scent down the hall and around a corner until we came upon three long rows of wooden tables topped with computers. With no windows on this side of the library, the temperature had dropped. A cacophony of the buzzing fluorescent lights and fingers striking keyboards filled the stale air.

"Here we are," she said, pulling out an empty wooden chair. She hunched over and clicked away at the keyboard. The library's home page filled the screen. "Just enter your library card number here."

I pulled Gran's card from my shorts pocket and keyed in the number.

I scanned the tabletops. There were no printers in sight. "How do I print?"

"After you send your print job to the printer named Library Copier . . ." She marched across the room, with me tailing her neon pink flats, to a huge copier tucked away in an alcove. "Then scan your library card. This logs you in to the copier, and then you can release your print job. The first three pages are free."

Tickled Pink demonstrated the process using her own card, and the screen showcased zero print jobs ready. Her finger pointed at, but never pressed, the print button.

"Come get me if you need anything." She scuttled off in a pink blur.

I settled into the chair's vinyl padded seat and faced the computer. The cursor blinked on the internet search engine screen, awaiting my instructions. Fig's list of symptoms ran through my head: Hershey breath, never enough water in his bowl, shrinking appetite, and Sleeping Beauty syndrome. Choosing few words, but being as specific as possible, was the best approach on a database like this. I typed "cat sweet breath, thirsty, not hungry, sleepy" and hit enter.

I gnawed on my nails. The screen blinked. After a second or two the results loaded.

The words "Feline Bad Breath" loomed in blue at the top. I clicked on the link. A zoomed-in picture of a cat's propped-open mouth with a tube shoved down his throat filled the screen. He was receiving a professional teeth cleaning. The photo left a bad taste in my mouth. The *Cat Fancy Pants* article covered noxious, putrid, foul, stinky, and even urine-smelling breath. But not one mention of sweet.

I moved on to the next article in the list. My energy

perked once I read the title: "Lethargy in Cats." I devoured every word. "Cats naturally sleep a lot, but excessive rest can be a sign of illness. . . . Other symptoms associated with causes of lethargy include: diarrhea, jaundice, difficulty breathing, hair loss . . ." But I was left feeling frustrated. The article hadn't mentioned any of Fig's other symptoms.

Releasing a heavy sigh, I returned to the results page. I saw the next link and sucked in my breath. It was an article from *Cat Fantastic* magazine titled "The Silent Cat Killer."

Reeling in my nerves, I pressed on, inhaling the first page. "Diabetes mellitus—commonly referred to as diabetes—is a costly, silent killer. This complex but common disease occurs when a cat's body either doesn't produce or doesn't properly use insulin."

Whoa. Cats could get that too? I thought only people got diabetes, and only when they ate too much junk food.

My body stiffened as I read the list of symptoms smack in the middle of the screen:

- excessive urination and thirst
- larger clumps in the litter box
- a decreased or ravenous appetite

- overweight/obese body or weight loss
- abnormal breath
- lethargy

The facts stared at me. Sir Fig Newton wore every sign of this illness. My stomach cramped. Fig was sick. *Disease* sick. My gut had been right.

I read all three pages. Twice. The article talked about the long-term complications that could result from diabetes: kidney disease, infections, and liver issues. There was even a picture of a cat who'd suffered nerve damage, his hocks flat on the ground, each like a broken, unlucky rabbit's foot. I gnawed on my bottom lip.

The article's only advice was to visit the vet immediately if your cat showed any of the symptoms.

I plopped my head onto the table. The facts overwhelmed me and wrenched my already aching belly. Sir Fig Newton was really sick. Going to the vet was expensive. All I could picture was Mom's glum face after finding out about Dad's pricey plane ticket, and Dad's crushed expression when he'd admitted that he didn't know when he could replace my broken phone. How would they look once I told them about Fig?

Finally I peeked over my folded arm. I pulled myself up and stared down the computer.

I sent the three-page article to the printer and hurried over to the large copier. After swiping Gran's library card, the screen displayed one job ready. I hit the print button. The copier wheezed, gears spinning to print my indisputable facts. When no papers appeared, I smashed the button again. The machine continued to grunt and grind. My nose wrinkled at a smoky smell.

I rapidly pressed the print button again and again, urging the machine to do its job. The smell grew stronger and more pungent. The copier responded with a strangled cough.

The tickled-pink librarian rushed toward me. "What's wrong?"

A single wrinkled page spat out of the copier. She turned off the machine and pulled open the tray, exposing jammed paper and a thin trickle of smoke. Her face scrunched up like a wad of bubble gum. Fanning the smoke aside, she muttered, "I've never seen it overheat like this."

I could feel the color draining from my face. Maybe I

should've explained that I was the reigning Short-Circuit Scientist, destroying anything and everything electric-powered. I'd tried telling that to Thomas after I'd accidentally destroyed his favorite video game, but that hadn't kept him from not talking to me for an entire week.

My hand shaking, I grabbed the single sheet. *What Is Dia* were the only words on the page, followed by a long black smudge. My indisputable facts had gone up in smoke.

10

GIVE UP THE FUNK

act: The odds of being struck by lightning this summer were one in five hundred thousand, and one in four million of being bitten by a shark, but it was 100 percent guaranteed that my Short-Circuit Scientist reign would ruin everything.

Pacing in front of the library waiting for Gran, I shaded myself from the sun under the roof overhang, but the air kept blowing gusts of hot breath in my direction. I tried not to panic. Sir Fig Newton had the silent cat killer, and my only proof had melted into extinction. And with all the commotion, I'd completely forgotten to check my email and update Thomas.

Gran's shiny green Oldsmobile pulled up. When I opened the passenger door, a blast of frigid AC air slapped my cheeks. A tune similar to the one from her living room, preaching "lean on the Lord," filled the car, this one with a creepy organ backdrop.

"How'd it go, Miss Mira?" Gran asked, turning the car onto the main road.

"Remember when I said that my summer sucks?" I huffed. "I was wrong. It's worse. This summer stinks like rotten eggs on a dead skunk."

Gran's hands tightened around the steering wheel, but she let my inappropriate-for-a-lady words slide.

"I was right. Fig is sick."

During the rest of the drive home, I described in detail my *Cat Fantastic* findings proving my theory, and then the printer making them sizzle up in smoke.

Thankfully, the tickled-pink librarian hadn't pressed charges, not that I'd done anything wrong on purpose. I couldn't help my allergy to electronic stuff. Gran gave the appropriate head nods and "uh-huhs" whenever I paused to take in a breath and calm my jittery nerves.

"The article said to visit the vet right away if your cat shows any symptoms," I said, my words tumbling out high-pitched and shaky. Maybe I should've emailed the article to my parents, but I hadn't told them anything about Fig. Maybe then they'd have thought *I* had diabetes and get extra worried.

The car slowed as we turned into Gran's neighborhood. A fat orange tabby lay on his back in the grass, his four legs sprawled out in all directions. He stretched his toe beans wide, with an expression of blissful calm. Was Fig enjoying a midafternoon nap? Devouring a bowl of kibble? Grooming his gray fur? Or had his litter clumps grown larger? Did his breath still smell sweet? And was he stuck in a comatose state?

"My life sucks worse than a greedy black hole." I slumped in my bucket seat.

Gran pulled the Oldsmobile into her driveway, butted against a lush green lawn on one side and bushes on the other. The bushes were just high enough and in a perfect rectangular shape to block her neighbor's "junkyard." Every time Gran's gaze drifted in that direction—a yard covered in half-clothed dolls, every sports ball imaginable, and patches of trampled grass—she mumbled a prayer to save their souls, or maybe her mood.

"Enough with the language," she said, turning off the engine. "And put away that pout."

I sucked in my lips.

"God don't like ugly." She leaned over and popped open the glove box, then handed me a napkin from McDonald's. "I know you're worried about your cat, Mira, but God doesn't give us more than we can handle."

I dabbed at my moist eyes, inhaling the faint scent of a greasy cheeseburger and fries. I wanted to argue that I didn't believe in God. Where's the proof? But Gran didn't tolerate ideas like evolution or the big bang theory, despite the evidence.

"Did I ever tell you about your dad and his fear of needles?" she asked.

I nodded with a heavy sigh. I'd heard the story of Dad fainting at the doctor's office when he was a teenager, probably more times than he'd actually fainted.

"Just the sight of a needle would send him facedown into a coma," Gran said with a chuckle. "He always stayed clear of me and my sewing machine. But your daddy survived, didn't he?"

I wasn't sure Gran was proving her point. Dad was *still* deathly afraid of needles. Getting Dad to take his annual flu shot was more difficult than getting his attention while the Marlins were playing.

Gran sat silently for a few moments, appearing deep in thought. Finally she said, "You know what, Miss Mira? I think I can help."

I looked at her hopefully. "Really?"

She slammed the glove box shut and climbed out of the car. I hustled my stride behind her heels clacking against the pavement toward the house. Viper greeted Gran at the front door with a high-pitched howl, and me with a seething hiss. He jumped in line as we strode down the hall, through the lemon-scented kitchen, and into the damp laundry room. His constant nips at my ankles sure made me miss my sweet Fig. I even missed those 5:40 a.m. wake-up calls. Gran unbolted the door, and we stood in the doorway leading into her garage, shadows and dark outlines lurking throughout.

She flipped the switch, and the darkness dissolved

into wobbly piles of dust-covered junk and crooked cardboard-box towers. Black garbage bags threw up mothballed clothes. Rusty hammers and screwdrivers of various sizes haphazardly decorated a wall. My eyeballs popped out of their sockets. A ton of ancient stuff filled the entire space.

I ran my fingers down the spines of various CDs housed in a metal tower at least four feet tall. With artists like Prince, Fishbone, and Parliament, these had to be Dad's old discs.

Whatever happened to "Cleanliness is next to godliness?" Gran was a closet pack rat! *This* must be where I inherited my "tidying up" skills from. Gran was just better at keeping her mess out of sight.

"Which issue, did you say?" Gran asked, scanning the Sharpie-labeled boxes.

"*Cat Fantastic*. 2013. I'm not sure what month." I tiptoed through the maze behind her.

"I started subscriptions to several feline periodicals, back when I had my Maine coons, and never canceled them." Viper whined, bumping his pointed snout against Gran's leg. "Please, Viper," she scolded. "Envy is not a virtue."

I snorted.

Gran shuffled over to another towering pile and removed the top two boxes. A dust cloud puffed into the air as she opened the bottom box, sending Viper into a sneezing frenzy. That would teach him to stick his curious nose where it didn't belong.

There was a whole mess of *Cat Fantastic* magazines, along with *Cat Fancy Pants, Essence,* and *Ebony.* I dug through the jam-packed box, my nose twitching. I didn't know what tickled worse: inhaling dust mites, or Viper's sharp whiskers poking into my bare leg. I scanned the table of contents in nine different *Cat Fantastic* magazines from 2013 until I spotted the words "The Silent Cat Killer." I flipped to the article's first page to make sure it was really there. The pang in my abdomen burst into glee.

"Thanks, Gran." I wrapped my arms tight around her thin waist. I was so giddy, I could have even snuggled up with Viper.

"Praise Jesus. God is good." Gran ruffled my loose curls. "Now no more whining about a rotten summer, Miss Mira."

* * * * * *

While Gran made herself a cup of tea, I sat at the kitchen table, staring at the *Cat Fantastic* magazine. A blue-gray cat with round copper eyes posed on the cover, his elegant stance twisting his husky frame. The words "Meet the Chartreux: French, Quiet & Cute" floated across the cat's image. Other cover lines included: *Seven Steps to a Thinner Mew*; *Five Places to Pet Your Cat without Losing a Limb*; and *The Latest Scoop on Litter*. But all I could think about was "The Silent Cat Killer."

My mind stressed over how to present the article to my parents. Sure, Dad was super upset that they couldn't replace my dead phone. And Mom had freaked out over a ridiculously expensive plane ticket. But taking Sir Fig Newton to the vet was a matter of life and death.

The stove kettle whistled, causing Viper to scurry from the kitchen. After pouring hot water into a delicate rose-covered cup, Gran settled into the chair next to me. She hummed along with one of her church choir songs softly playing on an old boom box.

I traced my finger over the cat on the magazine cover. There was nothing I could do for Sir Fig Newton until I was back at home, so I readjusted my focus to dragging my parents away from the event horizon with my mood-music hypothesis.

"Now that you've helped me prove that Fig's really sick," I said, "will you help me snap Dad out of his funk?"

Gran's face wrinkled with concern. "What do you mean?"

"The facts don't lie," I said as Gran repeatedly dunked her tea bag. I explained how Dad had been miserable since he'd lost his job, no matter how many times he claimed, "It's all good." And now he'd lost his childhood friend.

Gran sighed. "Every time I call, he always acts like everything's fine. Wish he'd come to me." She released the tea bag. "How can I help?"

"I'll be right back."

I raced to my room and returned with my backpack slung over my shoulder. I removed the stopwatch, notebook, pen, and iPod with the recreated playlist. I turned off Gran's church choir CD and searched the kitchen for a docking station.

"Where can I play this?" I asked, holding up my iPod.

Gran stared at me as if I'd asked whether aliens had just landed on Earth and appointed Garfield as the new purrsident of the United States, with Snoopy as his VP.

"What is that thing?"

"Never mind," I said, shaking my head. This was just a minor setback. Scientists encounter them all the time. All I needed was persistence and an ounce of creativity. "Give me one second."

I took off to the garage and hastily examined the tower of CDs. I snatched a few from the rack and returned to Gran in the kitchen. She cut her eyes at me.

"I'll play some songs. Then tell me your mood and let me take your resting heart rate."

Her face relaxed into normal. "Oh. Well, that's simple enough."

I nodded in agreement. "On a scale of one to ten, ten being the most stressful, rate your current stress level."

"Life is good, other than a granddaughter who never comes to visit." Her sharp tone held no hint of teasing. Gran sipped on her tea, her gaze unfocused. "I'd say a three."

Ignoring the personal jab, I jotted down her response. "What's your energy level?"

"An eight."

"How would you describe your current mood?"

She savored another sip. Her face was calm, but her eyes flickered as if searching for the right word. "Somewhere between content and complacent."

I took Gran's initial resting heart rate, counting a total of thirty-four beats for thirty seconds, and scribbled sixty-eight in my notebook.

"Pay attention to how you feel as you listen to the music."

I slipped one of the discs from the garage into the CD player and pressed the play button. A bass guitar's slow notes intertwined with a saxophone's glee, creating a jazz-funk, strut-like rhythm, soon joined by trumpets and drums. Gran pursed her lips as Parliament sang "Give Up the Funk."

After twenty seconds, I lowered the volume until Dad's favorite song faded into silence. I removed the CD and took Gran's pulse. Up a full ten beats. Even though a rapid pulse equaled excitement, it was pretty clear by Gran's expression that she was not happy.

"What's your stress and energy levels now?" I asked.

"Six and seven."

"And your mood?"

"Disturbed."

I stuck in another CD, this time from Gran's personal stack by the boom box. A church organ piped a shoulder-rocking beat, soon followed by Mahalia Jackson's deep, soulful voice belting "Oh Happy Day."

Eyes closed, Gran swayed from side to side, mouthing along with the song.

Just as I'd expected. Not only did a song's rhythm and tone affect one's mood, but it really came down to personal taste. Gran despised Dad's favorite song. But the moment she heard gospel, her mood lifted.

I couldn't wait to get back home. The *Cat Fantastic* article would convince my parents to take Fig to the vet, and then I'd make tailored playlists to get their feet tapping right out of their funk—far, far away from the event horizon. And like in the photo from our day spent at the Kennedy Space Center, my family, including Sir Fig Newton, would be happy again.

IN SPITE OF THE FACTS

Neither rain nor heat nor stomachache could keep Gran away from Sunday service. Her dedication to church was like my commitment to becoming the world's greatest scientist. Overhead fans wheezed against the heavy, hot air as Gran and I made our way down the aisle. We crept like an atom cloud shot by lasers—or barely at a snail's pace—as several folks slowed us down to say their hellos.

"Morning, Ms. Elmira."

"Tests came back benign, Ms. Elmira. God is great!"

"Hope to see you and your greens at next week's pot-luck, Ms. Williams."

Gran and her head nods came to a stop once her long-time friend, Miss Nora, approached.

"Another beautiful day, am I right?" Miss Nora said, pulling off her pink gloves.

"Every day I wake up is beautiful," Gran said, and chuckled.

"Well, look at you, Mira." Miss Nora flashed a huge smile, but before I could even respond, she turned back to Gran. "That granddaughter of yours is sprouting like a weed!"

The two of them gabbed for a good five minutes before we resumed our slow march. Finally we arrived at our destination and settled onto the wooden bench in the third row, by the aisle.

Mom, Dad, and I didn't go to church. Even though Dad was Baptist like Gran, he'd only gone while he was growing up. Now that he was "all grown," as Gran put it, he said he needed his weekends to relax. I think he just wanted to stay home and watch sports. Mom never went to church when she was a kid but said she believed in God.

That was a lie. I knew this for a fact, because that night when she received the phone call about Grandma Millie's accident, I overheard her and Dad. Mom said that Grandma had "sacrificed and struggled her entire life, and this just proves that there's no such thing as God."

And I believed Mom was right.

When I was little, I used to pray for small things that I really wanted, like a new bike or a Smarty Science Wiz Kit. Kind of like a backup plan to my letter to Santa Claus. Most of the time those prayers came through.

But when I prayed so hard for Grandma Millie to wake up from her coma, and those prayers went unanswered, I was convinced God was just another white dude with a fluffy beard that adults made up to make children be good.

There was one thing, however, that made coming to Sunday service with Gran totally worth it: gawking at the gobs of people strutting into church wearing their Sunday best. It was like a runway show with every color from the big Crayola box on parade. In a feathered hat and banana-yellow dress dragging past her feet, one woman waddled to her seat. Another polyester dress, this one in marshmallow white, sauntered down the aisle, topped with a ginormous hat decorated with a pink bouquet around the brim. The best was the balding guy in a plaid suit jacket, dark jeans, and shiny red sneakers that matched his bow tie.

Several heads turned as Gervean Campbell sashayed through the opened double doors, dressed in a perfectly fitted sapphire pantsuit and really high black heels. She flashed a blindingly white smile, as her manicured nails brushed a lock of relaxed hair behind her ear. She'd been the local news anchor for years, and seemed to know everything about everyone.

"Who does Miss Gervean Campbell think she is in that too-tight Gucci suit?" Gran huffed under her breath, staring daggers at the one celebrity at First Baptist Church. "We're in the Lord's house, for heaven's sake. Bet you it's a knockoff."

Gervean sat in the row across from us, and Gran kept muttering to herself. Guess even old people can have a nemesis.

I tugged at my scratchy collar. If there really was a God and he supposedly loved me as I was, which Dad claimed he did, I didn't understand why I couldn't wear my shorts and T-shirt. Gran insisted that it was our way of showing respect. She said it didn't matter if frilly dresses with green bows were not my thing.

My fidgeting continued when the congregation sang along with the choir, songs like the ones blasting in Gran's house and car. I tried to push away my restless mood by coming up with mental playlists for my parents. Of course, Dad's would include his favorite track by P-Funk. Gran had already said it was okay if I borrowed some of his CDs collecting dust in the garage. Mom's playlist would only have show tunes and movie soundtracks.

After the navy-robed singers settled into their tiered seats at the back of the stage, the crowd straightened as the pastor strutted into the spotlight. He had that confident swagger that you knew meant he believed he could convince a scientist the world was flat.

"Brothers and sisters." His voice, deep and upbeat, boomed through the church without a microphone. "Today we are going to talk about faith . . . in spite of the facts."

What? I stopped fidgeting. Facts were my life.

"Our God is bigger than the *facts*. He's not limited by the laws of nature, science, or the almighty dollar."

"Amen." Heads nodded. Hands waved in the air.

My jaw locked. I wanted to shout, *Ridiculous! The laws of science are solid. Try to not be held down by gravity, and see how high you rise. Can I get a "Darwin"?*

But I said nothing. I just sat there gritting my teeth.

"Let me tell you a story," the preacher said, gliding across the stage. "A story about a rabbi named Jairus, who pleaded with Jesus. 'My daughter is dying. Please come and put your hands on her so she'll be healed.'"

The pastor paused his stride and dabbed his white hankie at his brow. "Some people from the house of Jairus came and cried out, 'Your daughter is dead!'"

I sucked in my breath.

"Jesus told Jairus, 'Don't be afraid; just believe.'"

Believe in what? The girl was dead. My head swung in Gran's direction. Nodding her entire body, she hung on to the pastor's every word.

"At the home of the rabbi, Jesus took the girl's hand and said, 'Get up.'"

Random churchgoers jumped to their feet.

The pastor leaned forward. "Immediately the girl stood up and began to walk."

"Praise Jesus," voices shouted. Hands shot into the air.

I looked around the room in amazement. Who would want a zombie as a daughter? Sure, it was a good story, but so was my favorite TV show, *Doctor Who*. If time travel was for real, I'd be the first one to jump into the TARDIS police call box, or a tesseract or a wormhole, so I could travel faster than the speed of light. Did anyone follow up with this Jairus to make sure his kid didn't eat his brains?

"Do like Jairus and have no fear." The pastor's words were magnified by his flailing arms. "Be like Jesus and believe. Choose faith."

I scowled at the sweaty preacher, trying to dissect the thoughts in my brain. Sure, it would be nice for someone to swoop in and make everything all good. But I couldn't stop thinking about what Dad had told me, about facing your own battles. How could anyone think something totally unprovable would help them?

A hypothesis was one thing. But the truth lay in the facts.

I was so tangled in my thoughts that I missed that the service had ended. The organ music accompanied our walk down the aisle and out of the church. As we made our way to the parking lot, I asked Gran, "Do you really believe Jesus brought that girl back to life?"

"You missed the point, Miss Mira," Gran said. "It doesn't matter what I, the pastor, or anyone else thinks. What matters is what *you* believe. Do you have faith in your beliefs?"

I climbed into Gran's Oldsmobile and stared at the rows of headstones at the cemetery next door as I thought about her question. I believed in the theory of relativity and everything else I'd learned in Miss Kirker's classes. After testing different songs on Mrs. B and Gran, I believed that music could change one's mood. I also believed that once my parents saw the silent cat killer article with all of Sir Fig Newton's symptoms, they would get help for Fig.

While humming one of her choir songs, Gran pulled the car out of the church parking lot.

"Yes," I said finally, "I do have faith."

"Then you'll be able to get through whatever life hands you," Gran said. "Faith allows for possibilities."

She started to tap her finger on the steering wheel, waiting for the light to turn green.

Faith allows for possibilities.

The sentence tumbled around in my head. It was through observation and experimentation that scientists made new discoveries. If we were to stop asking questions, then how would we ever uncover the unknowns of the universe? Or find new truths? Even scientists didn't always agree. A long time ago scientists believed that light always traveled in a straight line. Einstein thought that space was curved and that light bent when it traveled. Many scientists hoped he'd be proven wrong. But after photographs of the 1919 total eclipse showed that light bent as it passed the sun, the facts proved without a doubt that Einstein was right!

Hmm. Maybe there was something to the pastor's story. Not the whole zombie part, but in having faith in what you believed, even when others didn't agree.

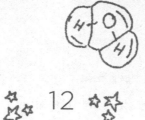

12

SKIN AND BONES

After dinner Gran and I sat on the plastic patio furniture on her back porch. Although the sun was slowly setting behind the treetops, the summer heat had no plans to pack it up for the night. Gran sipped on her iced tea, while my hands clamped around a sweating glass of lemonade. Ever since our car ride home from church, my brain couldn't stop examining the idea of faith without facts.

Mostly I kept thinking about all the stuff I believed in without any proof. Even before I'd found the cat-killer article, there had been many signs supporting my gut feeling that Fig was sick, so that didn't count. There were only three beliefs I could come up with:

I was going to be an astronomer, most likely an astrophysicist.

I was going to be an astronaut.

One day I'd be the greatest scientist that ever lived (after Einstein).

There were many other things that I really, really wanted, like to finally beat Tamika at the science fair or to be the first person to walk on Mars, but I couldn't say for a *fact* that I had total faith that these things would happen. I studied Gran's wise face, curious about her faith.

"Gran, what do you believe in?"

She set her glass on the patio table and gave me an odd look. "Is this related to our earlier conversation about the pastor's sermon today?"

"Mm-hmm." I nodded.

She drummed her fingers on the tabletop, her eyes distant as if she were deep in thought. After a few moments her fingers stopped moving and she smiled to herself.

"When I was your age, I believed in my mother, because she was the smartest person I knew and always put my needs first. In high school I could always depend on my music teacher to tell me the honest truth. And then there's my best friend of forty years, Miss Nora, always with a smile and a kind word.

"I may not trust her mac 'n' cheese . . ." Gran chuckled under her breath and then narrowed her eyes at me. "Don't you dare tell her I said that."

I quickly shook my head.

"But I do trust her with my life." Gran paused and took a sip of her tea.

"When I placed my trust in God, believing in something bigger than myself, that was the first time I had faith. I believed in something without proof. Whether in family, friends, or God, faith is my choice. Like Jesus told Jairus, 'Don't be afraid; just believe.'"

We sat there in silence as the sun fully vanished from the horizon. It was pretty quiet except for a sudden burst of canned laughter from the neighbor's TV and the occasional buzzing from an annoying mosquito.

"All righty, Miss Mira," Gran said, getting up from her

chair. "Time for my beauty rest. Don't stay outside too late, or these mosquitoes will eat you alive."

"Good night, Gran."

After the sliding door shut, I got up and wandered out into the yard, until I found the perfect spot near an orange tree. I lay in the grass and stared up into the night sky. I located what I believed to be Jupiter, glowing a bright orange. I held my finger in the air and connected the twinkling dots above the planet, tracing the Leo constellation. A backward question mark formed the lion's head and chest, and a triangle to the left represented the lion's haunches. It was my way of making the stars, and the unknown, feel within reach.

Questions started to fill my head as the grass tickled my ankles. Was there anything bigger than the universe? Were aliens out there? Would we ever reach the closest star? Even if I traveled for trillions of miles, I'd barely reach Proxima Centauri, the next closest star after the sun. The space between Thomas and me felt just as big.

I thought about the time when Thomas had stood up for me during third-grade recess. We'd been playing astronauts about to blast off into space, when this bully named Aaron had stomped over toward us and shouted, "Girls like you can't be astronauts."

"Can too!" I'd challenged with my hands on my hips.

"Your hair's so big, a helmet would never fit over it," he'd said, and snorted.

I'd lightly patted my bushy curls and frowned.

Thomas had quickly jumped in between us. "You're just jealous because NASA would never let you be an astronaut because they only allow team players," he'd said. "Plus, Mira's hair is so much cooler than yours."

Just like Gran, I too had people in my life who had my back. I realized that I hadn't conclusively proven that Mom and Dad would help with Sir Fig Newton after I presented the cat-killer article, but I knew that my parents always put me first. I could always depend on my favorite scientist, Einstein, of course. And I definitely trusted Thomas with my life, even if he couldn't tell a joke to save his. I was strong like miranium. I wasn't afraid. I believed.

My faith was in the facts. The indestructible, indisputable facts.

* * * * *

Monday evening couldn't get here fast enough. Although I loved Gran, I could stomach only so many *Black-ish* reruns and servings of collard greens.

"Thanks again, Gran," I said, clutching the *Cat Fantastic* magazine as I was about to jump into the passenger side of Mom's idling Toyota.

"Where do you think you're going?" she asked, hands on nonexistent hips, hovering by Mom's rolled-down driver's window. "Where's my sugar?"

"Sorry, Gran." I slunk around the car and planted a tight-lipped peck on her cheek.

"I hope she wasn't much trouble," Mom said to Gran as I buckled in.

"And *I* hope it won't be another five months before she visits again," Gran replied, her face stone-cold. Mom laughed hesitantly, her right leg bouncing.

Gran's expression softened as she leaned closer to the window. "You take care, Miss Mira. And remember"—she winked at me—"you can handle anything life dishes out."

I waved as the Toyota grunted out of the driveway.

"What was that all about?" Mom asked. She was

dressed in her gray suit, with matching bags under her eyes. Pretty much the same look as when she'd dropped me off at Gran's four days ago.

"Nothing." I shrugged.

The setting sun hovered over the rooftops, casting a yellowish-orange glow in the darkening sky. We drove past Gran's neighbor's junkyard, where some kid was pedaling his bike with a vengeance, and that same fat orange tabby was lounging in the grass. His fluffy tail swayed from side to side.

I'm coming home, Fig.

"Have a nice visit?" Mom rolled up her window as we turned onto the Highway 520 exit.

"Yup," I said. "How's Sir Fig Newton?"

"Oh, me? I'm just fine," Mom joked. "I see where I rank."

"I missed you too." It's just that *she* didn't show any signs of the silent cat-killing disease.

She nodded at the magazine in my lap. "What's that?"

My hand protectively hid the cover.

Mom had called every night during my time at Gran's. I'd drilled her on Fig's status, and she'd always responded with, "He's fine." Not once had I brought up my *Cat Fantastic* diagnosis, wanting to deliver the news in person. Mom wasn't an animal lover like Dad and me. She'd only agreed to a cat because she'd said they were self-cleaning, like an oven.

I flipped the magazine over. "Nothing," I said.

Mom launched into a one-sided conversation about her work stuff, but my worried mind struggled to tune in. The world whizzed by. Looming trees hugged the two-lane highway, and scattered billboards advertised MAKE WAVES. RON JON SURF SHOP—COCOA BEACH 38 MI; GOD, GIVE ME A SIGN; and CURIOSITY IS OUT THERE underneath the NASA logo. Even with my observational data and the magazine article, would my parents believe me?

Eventually Mom stopped chatting and switched on some boring talk radio station for the rest of the hour drive home. I inhaled deeply, thinking about what Gran and I had talked about yesterday, about not being afraid and having faith. But as I let out a shaky exhale, Fig's fate weighed on my shoulders.

"Home sweet home," Mom sang off-key as the Toyota chugged into the driveway.

"Fig!" I bounded through the front door. "I'm baa-ack."

My enthusiasm plummeted when he failed to trot, waddle, or even slink down the hall. For his entire five years and ten months, the only time Fig hadn't greeted me was when he'd been hiding under my bed because of lightning flashes and growling thunder. The air in no way wore a hint of rain.

I flew past Dad crashed on the living room sofa watching TV and burst through my bedroom door with an impatient, "Sir Fig Newton."

Curled in the center of my bed, Fig lifted his head with a questioning *Mm-hmm?* I rushed over and nuzzled my face into his gray fur. I picked him up, but his no-longer-so-heavy frame practically slipped from my grasp. My hands tightened to keep him from dropping to the floor.

My body shivered. I thought about the picture of the cat walking on his hocks in the *Cat Fantastic* magazine. I should've told my parents right away about all the things wrong with him. We should've already taken Fig to the vet.

I bolted down the hall, clutching Fig against my thundering chest, and planted myself in front of the TV. Sitting next to Dad, Mom gave a look that could have cracked Superman in half. But I remained strong, like miranium, ready to face her kryptonite.

"Mira," Dad said, waving his hand, "Anderson's up to bat."

"Mira," Mom said in that tone I'd usually not cross.

Holding out a limp Fig, I cried, "Sir Fig Newton has the silent cat killer."

Dad stopped struggling to see around me. "What?"

"Endless thirst, lots of pee, sweet breath. Fig has diabetes." The words flew out so fast, I wasn't sure that they made any sense. My body was shaking, yet I was stiff, like whenever Dad let me watch scary movies.

Fig let out a nervous yelp. I loosened my grip. No scary movie, failed experiment, or broken cell phone came close to the fear now pumping my heart at a hundred thousand beats per minute. I plopped Fig onto Dad's lap. "He's all skin and bones."

Dad sighed. His tired eyes locked with mine. "I'm sure everything's—" He stroked Sir Fig Newton. "Oh."

"What's wrong?" Mom leaned over.

"I can feel his spine." Dad frowned.

"I should've told you sooner." My voice cracked, and I slumped down onto the couch with my face in my hands. "If he dies, I'll never forgive myself."

"Mira, honey," Mom said with a sad smile, "everything's going to be okay. We'll take Sir Fig Newton to the vet and figure it out."

Dad nodded in agreement, unable to hide the worry on his face.

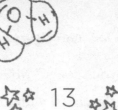

13

BARKS, WHINES, AND HOWLS

Fact: Pavlov's dog may have learned to salivate when hearing a ringing bell, but when a bell jingled as Dad and I entered the Brevard Animal Clinic, my poor skittish nerves were startled. We were greeted by a chorus of barks and meows from the patients scattered throughout the waiting area. Arctic AC temperatures numbed the tight space, keeping the not-so-fresh furry odors to a minimum.

Magazines and pamphlets were fanned across a side table: last month's issue of *Cat Fantastic*, several well-worn copies of *Bark & Bone's No More Itch: Get Rid of Fleas & Ticks*, and *Litter Box Hits and Misses*. A wooden plaque hung on the wall with VOTED BEST VET IN BREVARD COUNTY written in gold, next to a gigantic poster with an army general barking, SPAY OR NEUTER YOUR CRITTER!

I lugged the jumbo plastic carrier meant for a twenty-pound dog to an empty corner and set it on the tiled floor. An overexcited pug snorted and gasped, shoving his short-muzzled face against the crisscross-prison-barred door of Fig's cage. Fig released a strangled whimper and scuttled to the back of the carrier, then crouched into a tight ball.

I shoved my foot between the pug and the steel gate, hoping to slow Fig's heart a few beats closer to calm. Usually I loved greeting and meeting with all the furry creatures, but my mind was stuck on Fig and the grim possibilities my research had revealed. My thoughts were wound so tight that my temples pounded with a killer ponytail headache. Even my weekly phone call with Thomas this morning hadn't calmed me down.

Maybe I was one of those hypochondriacs, obsessing

over Fig's health. And no matter how many ways my mind dissected Fig's situation, my entire body continued to cramp in fear. My poor fingernails were chewed down to the nub.

After checking in with the receptionist, Dad settled into the chair next to me. "It's all good, Mira," he said, ruffling my curls. "Everything's going to be all right."

Thomas had said the same thing during our call, and those stupid words still didn't make me feel better. I wanted to believe in Gran's faith without any proof. Even more, I wanted to argue that no one could possibly know that everything would be fine, not 100 percent without a doubt for sure. But I nodded instead.

A door squeaked open, and the vet's assistant poked her head out. Her pumpkin-orange curls piled high on her head reminded me of the bride of Frankenstein, even without the lightning bolt streaks on each side.

The assistant's gaze rushed over her clipboard— my heart was pounding—before she called out in a cheesy-grits accent, "Peanut Wigglebutt?" My shoulders slumped. The snorting pug tugged its human toward the carrot-top lady, grunting with each step. I bounced in my chair. The minutes crawled by as the assistant continually announced the next four-legged patient: "Shakespurr" (a hissing tabby) . . . "Snickerdoodle" (a strutting cinnamon-colored toy poodle) . . . "Diva" (a nervous bulldog wearing a diamond-encrusted collar). With each name called, my anticipation deflated with a heavy exhale.

I glanced over at a bulletin board on the opposite wall crammed with photographs of all kinds of pets. I swallowed hard. To the right were the words: "To our friends and family who have crossed the Rainbow Bridge. We love you. We'll miss you." Underneath were pictures labeled "Fluffy—June 21," "Muffin—December 14" . . . My vision blurred. With microscopic shakes of my head, I muttered, "No, no, no." Fig would NOT end up—

"Sir Fig Newton?"

My head snapped up. The vet assistant threw me and Dad a lightning-quick smile.

Dad grabbed Fig's cat carrier, a pathetic "maow" drifted out, and we followed the vet lady and her soaring curly do down the hall. She ushered us into an unoccupied all-white room with a set of cabinets and a big scale on top of a table.

"What brings Mr. Sir Fig Newton in today?" the vet assistant purred.

"He has the silent cat killer," I said.

Her eyes widened, and she turned to Dad for assistance. He sighed. "Diabetes. We think."

She nodded. Her pen clicked away against the clipboard as I recited the list of symptoms Fig had shown over the last week.

"Let's get him onto the scale."

She knelt on the concrete floor and unlocked the door to Fig's carrier.

"C'mon, big fella," she cooed.

Fig performed his interpretation of a disappearing act—crouching perfectly still.

The assistant reached her long, bony arms inside and dragged out a limp, defeated Fig. His lime-green eyes pleaded with me to save him. My heart shattered, and I snatched my glance away, ashamed that when he needed me most, I didn't have his back.

The vet assistant plopped him onto the scale and held her hands on either side of his shivering body without touching, trying to keep him in place. The needle zoomed up and wavered between fourteen and fifteen pounds. Once the needle settled, she scratched away on her clip-board, while Fig hurtled off the scale, dashing back to the safety of his carrier.

"Dr. Spires will be with y'all shortly," she said.

Muffled barks, whines, and howls rushed into the room as the door closed behind her. Dad paced the cramped space, hand-picking his 'fro. I blew on my cold hands. Time was at a standstill, except for the relentless ticking of the wall clock.

"I'm sorry you haven't found a new job yet, Dad," I blurted, shoving my chilled fists into my pockets. His pacing skidded to a jerky halt, and I suddenly felt embar-rassed, not sure why I'd said that. Maybe I felt guilty for pressing pause on helping Dad out of his funk.

"Thanks, Mira," he said with a grim smile.

The tick-tick-tick took over again, disturbing the awk-ward silence.

Finally Dr. Spires burst into the room with a boom-ing, "Welcome, welcome. So." His eyes grazed over the opened file in his hand. "Based on his recent symptoms and—wow—a twenty-two percent drop in his weight since last time, there is indeed a strong possibility that Sir Fig Newton has diabetes."

The vet dragged poor Fig out of his safety zone again and plunked him onto the exam table. He wheeled out the stool and settled down, poking and prodding Fig's trembling girth.

"Tell it to me straight, Doc. What are Fig's chances?" I asked.

Dr. Spires's mustache twitched. He had that look where you just knew he had a ton of hard information to share but was having a difficult time passing it on, probably because he thought I couldn't handle it.

"I've seen a number of pets live long, healthy lives with diabetes," he said.

A number? His words weren't unraveling my twisted tummy. Ten, fifty, one hundred and one, those were all numbers. So was zero. Where were the facts?

"Be specific," I pressed.

"Mira," Dad said.

"Specific?" He pressed a stethoscope against Fig's heaving chest. "Well, one in two hundred fifty domestic cats currently develop diabetes, usually in midlife or older. Researchers have concluded that excess body weight due to overeating, physical inactivity, or both often contributes to the disease. Cats newly diagnosed usually . . ."

Pulling back each of Fig's ears and peeking inside, Dr. Spires babbled on about chemical waste and blood and dysfunction. He never paused, the words spilling like overheated water from a beaker. Every so often he made eye contact with Dad, then me.

". . . Ketoacidosis . . . blah, blah, babble . . . fructosamine test . . . yak, yak, burble . . . chronic hyperglycemia . . . gush, surge, gurgle . . ."

I drowned in the flood of technical jargon.

"Right now, however," Dr. Spires continued, throwing me a lifeline, "we need to do some tests and wait on the results before knowing Fig's exact situation."

The vet got up from the stool and dug through the cabinet drawers, prompting Fig to make his second escape of the day. Actually, his third if you counted the twenty minutes it took to coax him out from under my bed and lock him up in his plastic carrier.

"Here's some detailed information to take home with

you." Dr. Spires held out a pamphlet, flashing a reassuring smile.

The glossy cover had a picture of a young boy playing fetch with his chocolate lab and the title *You and Your Pet Living with Diabetes*. It was like swallowing bittersweet cough syrup.

"Since it's late in the day, we'll just keep Sir Fig Newton overnight."

My eyes darted to Fig hiding inside the carrier.

"We'll do X-rays, a diagnostic profile, test his urine and blood for sugar levels, and check his thyroid," Dr. Spires continued. After bending over and locking the metal door, he hoisted the carrier to his side like a briefcase. "We'll call tomorrow when he's ready to be picked up, and then discuss next steps."

Everyone filed out of the room. Dad headed out front while I paused in the doorway. Dr. Spires strode down the corridor, my best furry friend howling the entire way, until they disappeared past swinging doors. Would Fig be included in the vet's number of long-lived survivors, or would his picture end up on the bulletin board with his name and a near-future date scribbled underneath?

The knots in my stomach tightened.

I opened the pamphlet and scanned the words. A bolded question headed every section: *What is diabetes? What causes it? What are the symptoms? How is it treated? What is the prognosis?* My eyes landed on the first sentence in the final paragraph.

There is no cure for diabetes.

I looked back toward the doors at the end of the hall. I wanted to push my way through and shout at the pet doctor and yank on his twitchy mustache. He'd said nothing about there being no cure. But the last thing Fig needed was an agitated doctor. I hurried down the hall, away from the one furry being in this entire world who depended on me most, and caught up with Dad standing at the receptionist's desk.

"The bill comes to $439.50," she said.

Whoa, that was a *lot* of money.

Hugging my aching belly, I bit my lip. I felt awful. After the broken phone and Dad's expensive plane ticket, I didn't want to make things worse for Mom and Dad.

Dad's face went from brown to pale to green in less than a tenth of a second. He fumbled with his wallet and stared at his silver credit card like he was going to upchuck.

"Sir?" the receptionist said.

After another uncomfortable moment Dad finally handed over the card. Ruffling my curls, he said that same phrase he'd been saying since he'd lost his job.

"It's all good, Mira."

This time it was more like he was trying to convince himself.

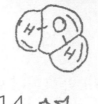
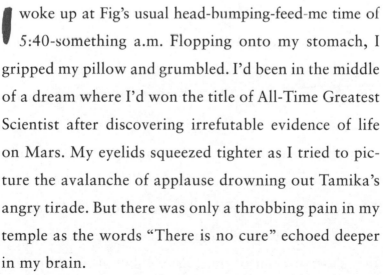

14

THERE IS NO CURE

I woke up at Fig's usual head-bumping-feed-me time of 5:40-something a.m. Flopping onto my stomach, I gripped my pillow and grumbled. I'd been in the middle of a dream where I'd won the title of All-Time Greatest Scientist after discovering irrefutable evidence of life on Mars. My eyelids squeezed tighter as I tried to picture the avalanche of applause drowning out Tamika's angry tirade. But there was only a throbbing pain in my temple as the words "There is no cure" echoed deeper in my brain.

Forcing myself upright, I caught the outline of Fig's hooded litter box. My chin quivered.

I dragged myself to the kitchen and flipped on the light. Despite the harsh glow, my world still felt dim. I dumped cereal into a bowl. Fig's empty food dish stared at me from the floor, piling on more pangs of guilt. Poor Fig was locked in a metal cage, smothered with strange smells, and surrounded by furry howling inmates, while I sat here having breakfast.

I pushed the bowl away. My mind needed something to do.

According to the pamphlet from the vet, *You and Your Pet Living with Diabetes,* the top three treatments were blood-sugar testing, insulin shots, and changing their diet. The fourth was exercise. I might not have been able to run out and buy Fig different food, but I was still the greatest scientist. I could make him work for it.

In the eat-in area of the kitchen, I spent over an hour constructing an elaborate obstacle course and placed Sir Fig Newton's food dish at the end. I stood back, reviewing my work. Even though Fig had lost a lot of weight in a short amount of time, he couldn't afford to gain it all back again. The thought *There's no cure for diabetes* returned. Why would anyone name a disease so that the first syllable was the word "die"?

I trudged into the living room and put *Beakman's World* into the old, dusty DVD player. It had been Dad's favorite show when he was a kid. He'd been excited to share it with me after I'd told him I wanted to be the world's greatest scientist, after Einstein, of course. It was no *Project Mc²*, but the experiments were pretty cool. Maybe reliable science could obliterate my worry.

I plopped onto the sofa. As I pressed play, the TV screen filled with Beakman wearing his green lab coat, the same lime green as Fig's eyes, and his dark hair teased toward outer space. He held a bowling ball, attached to a cable that hung from the ceiling, right in front of his nose.

It was my favorite episode, the one about the law of conservation of energy. By pulling the ball back in front of his face, a certain amount of energy had been placed into the ball. Beakman wanted to prove that if he let go, the ball wouldn't swing back past the point where he'd first held it.

I sank deeper into the sofa. For the first time, Beakman

and his assistants didn't make me laugh. Not even a slight grin.

Beakman released the ball. Like a pendulum it swung away from his face—down, down, down, then up, up, up—and then leisurely switched direction. Beakman clamped his eyes shut.

I turned the TV off and sighed. I already knew how it ended. Fact: The bowling ball halted right where it had started, in front of Beakman's nose, and then turned to swing back away again.

There is no cure. It's all good. No cure. All good. No. Good.

The landline phone rang, finally silencing the chatter in my brain. I rushed to answer it.

"Miranium," Thomas's voice sounded weird and tinny.

It wasn't the voice I was hoping to hear. "Hey. Didn't we just have our call?"

"I know, I know. I can't talk long, but I wanted to make sure everything's okay. How's Sir Fig Newton?"

My shoulders relaxed a little. "We're still waiting to hear from the vet, but he probably has the silent cat killer."

I told him all about the diabetes but didn't say anything about there being no cure. I had to keep strong, because miranium was indestructible. We talked for a few more minutes, or rather, Thomas gushed for a few minutes about his recent trip to the Lincoln Memorial. Then, of course, a joke.

"What do you give a sick lemon?" Thomas said.

"Don't know." My voice flattened.

"Lemon-aid."

My mood remained deflated. "Funny."

"Sorry about Fig," Thomas said.

"Thanks, and thanks for calling."

"That's what best friends are for."

Although I appreciated Thomas trying to cheer me up, my stress level remained stretched at one gigaparsec, about 3.26 billion light-years long. Not wanting the words from the vet's pamphlet to return, I found myself doing the unthinkable: cleaning my room.

And I mean for-reals clean. Dusting shelves (with books and stuff actually removed), changing the sheets, and vacuuming up every last crumb of litter wherever it didn't belong. I even filled a trash bag of clothes for Mom to donate.

The entire time, my ears strained, listening for the vet's call. By noon the phone still hadn't rung. I sat on my made bed, body bouncing, teeth clenched. My eyes flicked over the room. I needed something to calm my nervous twitch. I needed to get out of the house.

"Dad," I called out, dragging myself down the hall. "I'm gonna go ride my bike."

"Don't be too long," he yelled back.

I lugged my bike out of the garage and sped down the sidewalk, whipped by the breeze in the blistering sun. Our neighbor Mr. Spencer was out mowing his lawn and threw a nod in my direction. I nodded back and pedaled on.

I turned down the next block, whizzing past the cookie-cutter houses painted in one of three shades: bitter brown, sour cream, or sullen yellow. My brain scrambled for a hip-wiggling rhythm to force my heartbeat racing into joy. I started humming a fun, funky beat, but my mood remained bleak.

Without thought I circled back around and stopped my bike at the familiar old oak tree at the end of my block, its far-reaching limbs casting much-appreciated shade. Across the street was Thomas's old home.

Something was off. The house didn't look right. The smell of freshly cut grass tickled my nose. The house no longer vacant, the front porch was now decorated with hanging baskets of little pink flowers and white wicker furniture. The naked basketball hoop was gone.

The bright red FOR SALE sign had vanished too.

The front door swung open, but I couldn't make out anyone. Just dark fingers wrapped around the red door's edge. A muffled voice said something about ". . . be back. I know, I know. . . . won't forget . . . sheesh."

And then *she* stepped out onto Thomas's front porch. Her black kinky curls fanned around the familiar face like swirling hurricane clouds. Flower behind her ear. Anger sizzled my skin from my scalp to my short, stubby toes.

Tamika Smith had invaded Thomas's house.

15

ACORNS AND OTHER BOMBS

Fact: When your nemesis moves into your best friend's house and you discover it on the same day you're waiting to find out if your furry friend has the silent cat killer, your heart rate reaches top speed like race cars at the Daytona 500.

Standing across the street from Thomas's house, I felt my blood boil to a sizzling 212 degrees Fahrenheit, bringing heat to my cheeks and fingertips. How dare Tamika step her stank feet inside his house? She didn't belong here.

Steadying myself against the oak tree, I yanked a handful of acorns off a low branch. I imagined pulling back my hand, taut like a slingshot, and then launching the hard-shelled bombs at my rival. In an instant Tamika would be swallowed in a poof of thick smoke and transported to another dimension, leaving only her silly fake flower charred on the driveway.

"Hey, *El*mira. What are you doing?"

My attention snapped back to reality. Tamika faced me, her bright white flower tucked behind her ear.

"Me?" I spat. My fist tightened around the acorns. "What are *you* doing? In that house?"

Tamika followed my gaze. "We just moved in."

"But that's . . . that's Thomas's house." My fist unfolded, and the acorns fell to the ground with a symphony of plinks.

Some microscopic part of me had thought that as long as the FOR SALE sign sat in the front yard, there was still a chance that Thomas could, *would*, move back home. But now my brain shot back with that same *There's no cure* gloominess. I sat down on the curb, fingers trembling.

"Hey." Tamika's hand touched my shoulder, her voice no longer poking at my wounds. She actually sounded scared. "Are you okay?"

Our eyes met. She was frowning.

"C'mon, let's get you inside," Tamika said. She guided me toward Thomas's—I mean, *her* house. "You need orange juice, stat. Whenever my uncle used to get the shakes, OJ would fix him right up. That or honey or hard candy."

We went through the red front door like I'd done a million and one times before, but this time everything was different. No pile of sneakers that never made it to the closet. No Mrs. Thompson bustling around cleaning and cooking or in her favorite spot, on the blue sofa glued to her favorite soap, *Days of Our Young and Restless Lives*, or whatever it was called. The white walls were now painted beige, and instead of the big comfy sofa, stiff chairs sat alongside a cement-looking couch balancing on tiny wooden legs. It was spotless like Gran's house, but instead of smelling Lysol, I caught a whiff of dryer sheets, the summer-breeze kind.

Tamika led me into the kitchen.

"Forget something, T?" The woman standing at the counter was an older version of Tamika, dark-skinned with big hair, only no weird flower. "Oh, who's your friend?"

My nose wrinkled. Not the word I would use.

Tamika ignored her mom and bolted toward the fridge. I rolled my eyes.

"Mira." I offered my hand.

"You mean, *the* Elmira?" Her gold bangles clanked as she shook my hand. "I'm Tamika's mother, Mrs. Smith. I've heard so much about you. You're the great scientist T always talks about."

I faltered. Knowing Tamika, she'd probably complained about my campaign to overtake her first-place science fair domination.

Mrs. Smith gasped as she clamped her hand over mine. "You're shaking like Jell-O."

Tamika held a glass under my nose. "Imbibe this."

Mrs. Smith wore a somber smile. "We'd always feed my brother orange juice whenever he got the shakes. He called it his *magic elixir*." Her eyes went distant. "Diabetes is no joke."

"The silent cat killer." I nodded.

"Never heard it called that before," Mrs. Smith said. Her sad gaze locked with Tamika's. "My brother was diagnosed with diabetes three years ago."

"Is he okay?"

"Unfortunately, he passed away last year."

My grip tightened around my glass. I was afraid it would slip and fall onto the tile and shatter into a million pieces. "I-I'm sorry," I stammered out.

Tamika started rambling on about STEM Girls camp. With everything going on with Sir Fig, I'd completely forgotten that camp was starting next week.

"I wonder what we'll be doing this summer," Tamika said. "I hope we do another build-and-launch-your-own-rocket competition like last year."

I gulped down the orange juice, with both Tamika and her mom staring at me like Dad does at the laptop all day. The last time Tamika and I had stood this close, she'd been trying to poison me with not-spicy chicken soup and gather science fair intel. This was no longer Thomas's house. I had to get out of there. Away from enemy territory. Although, the OJ did taste pretty good.

"Thanks for the OJ, but I've got to get home." I set my empty glass on the counter and raced outside.

Their *magic elixir* might have ended my quivers and shakes, but a wicked sadness was brewing inside. I climbed onto my bike and pedaled toward home.

"Mira!" Mom's voice called. "We're home."

I ran out to the living room at the speed of light. I'd wanted to get Fig from the vet myself, but by the time the doctor had called, Dad had said it made more sense for Mom to pick him up on her way home from work.

Sir Fig Newton tiptoed out of his carrier, his pace slow and dazed, instead of making his usual dash to safety. I hugged him tight, his fur smelling like a mix of dogs and vet chemicals, pungent and sterile. He squirmed and whined, but I only squeezed harder. After a few more seconds of wrestling, Fig finally wriggled free and head-bumped my ankle, a sign that he'd missed me too.

"Come join us, Mira," Mom said, patting the spot at the dining room table next to her and Dad.

Oh no. A conversation at the table always equaled a change in barometric pressure. Stormy weather. Nothing good came from sitting at the dining table, but I plopped onto the edge of the hardwood chair between them anyway.

Mom tapped her fingers on the side of a steaming mug. "Turns out you were right, Mira. Sir Fig Newton has diabetes."

"You were right" were words you lived to hear your parents say, but Fig's official diagnosis was nothing to celebrate.

I took a deep breath. "What's next?" I asked.

Mom and Dad exchanged worried looks.

"What?" I tried to catch Mom's eyes, but she just stared into her mug. "What aren't you telling me?"

Fig nudged against my leg with a pathetic "meow" and settled on top of my sock-covered feet.

Dad cleared his throat. "Mira, you know things have been . . . different since I lost my job."

"Yeah, Mom's gone all day and now you're at home. And neither of you are happy anymore."

Dad coughed again.

"But it's all good, right?" My pleading eyes switched back and forth between Mom and Dad. "Mrs. Branson and Gran said you just have to have faith." Although I still thought belief without scientific support was suspicious, it felt like the right thing to say.

Dad smiled weakly. "It will be, someday. But until then, we don't have enough money for extra expenses."

My arm hair rose. "But Mom's working."

"Yes, sweetie," Mom said, "but it only goes so far."

"Mira," Dad said, "we can't afford the treatment for Fig's diabetes."

My brain freaked out.

I closed my eyes. If only I had access to ancient books at the library, like Doctor Strange. Then I could reverse time and prevent the ginormous star from exploding, so my family wouldn't be swallowed by a stupid black hole. Dad would have his old job back. Mom would go back to dressing up as Mary Poppins or Princess Leia, anything except a stuffy suit. Thomas would still live down the street. And Sir Fig Newton would be his heavy-duty self, napping and eating the days away.

I opened my eyes. I was still at the dining room table. Fig still lounged on my feet. His purring heightened my nerves. He had no idea how serious things were.

"But you said it was all good!"

Dad's eyes began to water. I was shocked. Although I was sure he'd cried before, like when his eyes were blood-shot after his best friend had died, Dad had never shed *real* tears in front of me.

"I know, Mira girl, but I was wrong," he said softly.

I got up and paced. There had to be some way. "We can use my allowance." I could do without five dollars a week, but I couldn't live without helping Fig get well.

"That's very sweet of you, Mira." Mom squeezed my hand. "But insulin shots and weekly blood-sugar testing and prescription food, it all costs a lot. And there's no guarantee he'll get better."

"How much? Be specific," I pressed.

"Much, much more than your allowance."

"What about Gran? She always gives me birthday and Christmas money. Maybe she can give it to me early."

"Mira, your dad and I have already discussed this at length. There's just not enough money in our budget, and Gran is already helping with other things."

"Did you even ask her?" My voice jumped an octave. Startled, poor Fig limped out of the room.

"Mira," Dad said.

"It's not like I'm asking for a phone."

"We know this is difficult to understand," Mom said, "but it's out of our hands."

"So, what? You're just going to let poor Fig get sicker and sicker until . . ."

The thought mangled my insides.

"You know Mom and I love Fig very, very much." Dad turned his sad gaze toward Mom.

Mom didn't say anything for longer than I could stand. Suddenly she grabbed my hands. "If we could, we would pay for his treatment, but . . . The vet thinks it would be best, and so do we . . ." She paused and snatched a glance with Dad. When she didn't continue, Dad finished her sentence.

"We're going to find Sir Fig Newton a new home."

16

EVERYTHING WAS NOT ALL GOOD

For a moment I couldn't even speak. Or move.

"What if I were the one who was sick?" I yelled at Mom and Dad. "Would you give me away too?!"

I tore down the hall and slammed my bedroom door shut. I didn't want to hear any more excuses. My parents had lied to me. They'd said it was all good. But everything was *not* all good. We'd taken a detour past all right and crashed head-on into my-life-is-officially-over territory.

I snatched the picture frame from my dresser and removed the photo, the one at the Kennedy Space Center in front of the space shuttle *Atlantis*. My glare bored into my parents' image. My jaw clenched. I grabbed a Sharpie from my desk. I ground the marker over Mom and that ridiculous *Star Trek* costume. Soon there was nothing left but a petite black blob. My skin boiling, I moved on to Dad. With each stroke the marker squeaked, obliterating his pressed khakis, blue button-down, and wide smile.

My jaw relaxed at the sight of the black holes that had swallowed my parents whole. But my peace was temporary. My gaze landed on Fig in my arms in the photo, and my heart broke all over again.

My parents were giving away Sir Fig Newton.

I left the photo on the desk and collapsed onto the bed. My fists pounded on the mattress. My legs kicked. The more I raged, the more friction and heat overwhelmed me. My body was like a shuttle reentering the Earth's atmosphere, hitting against particles of air and facing temperatures of three thousand degrees Fahrenheit. Maybe if I cried, the blaze would lessen. But my rage had caused a dam, trapping the tears inside.

There was a soft knock at the door. Mom entered

without an invitation. Sir Fig Newton slunk in behind her and jumped onto the bed. He gave me a look and then plopped down near my feet, just out of reach.

"Dinner's ready," Mom said.

I flipped over, my back to her face.

"Oh my," she gasped. "This room is clean."

I could hear her poking around, but I just kept staring at the wall.

"Like, spic-and-span clean." She whistled.

I'd completely forgotten about all the hard work I'd done this morning. That was an eternity ago.

"I've never seen it look so good. Not since the day we moved in, anyway."

Silly jokes were not going to soften me up. "Leave me alone."

"Mira, honey . . ." Mom sighed. "I know you're hurting right now. And that you're mad at Daddy and me, and you have every right to be. But giving Fig up for adoption is the best solution. We love you and Fig and—"

"Just leave me alone." I shot upright and gave Mom laser eyes. "You never wanted Fig in our family. I wish we could give *you* away instead."

Mom's pale cheeks highlighted with pink.

I leapt off the bed and stormed past Mom, down the hall, and out the front door. This time she didn't call after me. I jumped onto my bike, still dumped in the front yard, and pedaled hard with no destination in mind. Einstein once said, "Life is like riding a bicycle. To keep your balance, you must keep moving."

I circled the block, over and over, the houses and trees and cars a watery blur. I continued drifting down the same familiar streets, my body wobbly, my mind still out of balance, until I found myself parked in my neighbor's driveway. There was nowhere else to go. Gran was too far. Thomas's old house had been invaded. And Thomas himself was out of reach. Mrs. B would have to do.

I hesitated at the front door, wishing I were there to talk about the Andromeda Galaxy or the new Mars rover. Mrs. B had always been there for me, ready to volunteer as one of my test subjects for my experiments or answer all my questions about space. I just hoped she could help me now.

"Mira?" Mrs. Branson answered the door with Sabrina snug against her chest.

"My parents are big fat liars," I sobbed. "They said everything was good. But it's not."

Mrs. B ushered me inside and cleared a space for me on the couch. "What's going on?"

I inhaled deeply, and in one very long and hot breath explained everything that had happened over the last week. Fig's troubling symptoms. My investigative skills uncovering that Fig had diabetes, and the vet's confirmation. There not being enough money to take care of him. And then the worst of the worst.

"My parents are giving Sir Fig Newton up for adoption."

We sat in silence, except for the sound of Sabrina's satisfied hums as she sucked on her bottle.

"I know how much you love Sir Fig Newton. And how hurt and sad you must be feeling right now, Mira, but . . ." Mrs. Branson paused, switching Sabrina to the opposite arm. "This is really hard on your parents, too."

I shook my head. "Fig already has a home."

"Think about it from your dad's point of view. He lost his identity when he lost his job. I'm sure he misses it, just like how I miss making space shuttles. I'll be going back to work soon, but he's not sure when he'll find something new. He always did everything for you and your mother and Fig, and right now he's no longer able to."

I folded my arms tight. My anger was still solid like miranium.

"Imagine," Mrs. Branson said, "if you were no longer able to do your experiments. Or ask any more questions about the universe. How would that make you feel?"

I didn't budge. Who knew what I'd do if someone took that away from me? But it didn't change the fact that my parents were giving away Fig.

"Remember," Mrs. Branson continued, "your house, food, clothes, it all costs money. Everything's different when there's a little one." She nodded to Sabrina. "They have to put your needs first. Over Sir Fig Newton's. No matter how much it hurts you and them."

My arms dropped to my sides. Sure, they were trapped in the void's gravitational pull too. Dad out of work, Mom crunching numbers. But that couldn't come close to the pain burrowing in my chest.

"Who knows?" Mrs. B said. "Maybe Fig will end up with a family that'll let you come visit." She smiled as she laid Sabrina belly-down across her knees. She lightly patted her baby's back with her palm, her messy ponytail bobbing along. Mrs. B was only trying to help, but it wasn't working. If Thomas were here, he'd know what to do.

Thomas had only seen me cry once. Back in March, I'd lost the science fair for the fourth year in a row to my nemesis, Tamika. He hadn't made fun of my tears and instead had convinced me that I really would win first place next year. Thomas would understand. He'd take my side and help me come up with a plan to save the day.

"Mrs. B, do you have a best friend?" I asked.

"Mm-hmm. My sister."

"But isn't she all the way in Miami?"

She nodded. "The distance can be tough, but we work around it with phone calls, emails, and visits. Didn't your best friend just move?"

"To DC. It's been three weeks. It's hard not having him here."

Sabrina burped, followed by a dribble of milky spit.

"Good girl," Mrs. Branson cooed, wiping Sabrina's chin. "I completely understand. Whenever something big happens in my life, good or bad, my sister is the first person I want to share it with."

"Yeah. I could really use my best friend right now."

Mrs. Branson gazed down at Sabrina, cradled against her chest. "Would you like to use my phone?"

I looked up at her and smiled for the first time all day. "Can I, Mrs. B? I swear I won't be long."

"Take all the time you need," she said, and nodded toward the cell on the end table.

With a deep breath, I dialed Thomas's number. My pulse was racing like Mrs. B's heart rate when I was testing my mood-music playlist. Just to hear his voice would help.

After several rings there was a pause, followed by Thomas's familiar voicemail greeting.

"Hey, it's Thomas. Knock, knock. Who's there? . . . Not me! So, leave a message."

The ache was worse than when the judges had announced my second-place status. I set the phone back on the table and slumped onto the couch.

"No answer?" Mrs. Branson asked.

I shook my head. "What do you do when you can't reach your sister?"

Mrs. B held Sabrina up before her and nuzzled her

head into Sabrina's exposed tummy. "I hug this little one."

I sighed. Usually I'd do the same with Fig. His constant purr and head bump always kept me calm. But that wouldn't save him.

I left Mrs. B's and lingered in front of my house, not wanting to go inside. I dug my sneaker into the dirt, crumpling a patch of brown grass. If Thomas were here, what would he do?

He'd crack a really silly joke, trying to make me smile. He'd poke me in the shoulder and say those same words I'd fed to him whenever he'd get sick of his shots missing the basket. "Winning means never giving up." Thomas would remind me that nothing could knock me down because I was made of miranium, and that I was too stubborn to let anything keep me from saving Fig. And then I'd say that I preferred the word "persistent."

My sneaker dragged across the sidewalk, leaving a streak of dirt.

My thoughts raced back to March, after losing the science fair. I'd really thought that my model of a black hole to help visualize how it could "bend" space-time would win first place. Thomas had claimed that I'd already won, because in spite of my second-place reign, I kept showing up and doing what I loved.

"C'mon, Miranium," he'd said. "You're the greatest scientist in the universe."

I'd finally smiled, wiping my cheeks dry. "After Einstein, of course."

Now I marched toward the front door. The facts: Fig was still at home, where he belonged; insulin could help him get better; treatment cost more than my allowance. But the most important truth: I wasn't giving up on Sir Fig Newton.

17

THERE'S NO GUARANTEE

I busted back into the house, a determined scientist on a mission. I would never give up on Sir Fig Newton. Mom and Dad sat at the dining room table in silence, except for the clinking of forks and knives against their plates. The tension wasn't from Dad's very sloppy joes.

I slunk my way toward the table, eyes glued to my sneakers.

"Mom, Dad." I forced myself to face them head-on. "I'm sorry."

Dad stopped chewing. Mom's fork clanked onto her plate. They gaped at me.

Then I remembered what I'd said to Mom: "I wish we could give you away instead."

I turned to her and bowed my head. "I mean it. I really am sorry."

Mom nodded, her cheeks still flushed.

I pushed on through the guilt.

"I know that you don't want to hurt me or Sir Fig Newton."

Fig slogged into the room with a soft "mew" and then rubbed up against my leg. I scooped him up and positioned his head to point toward Mom. "So, I have a proposal for you both," I said, and then turned so that Fig's wide-eyed stare bored into Dad.

"Please, please, *please* just give me one month to figure out how to pay for Fig's treatment." I nuzzled Fig's belly as his entire body pulled away in protest. "I can't give up on him."

"Mira," Mom sighed, "it could take up to ten visits to get his blood sugar in line. We'd need enough money to cover expenses for *at least* three months."

"We're talking about a lot of money," Dad said.

I nodded as Fig wriggled from my grasp and landed on the floor with a loud thud. "How much do we need?"

Mom got up from the table, the wooden legs of her chair scraping across the floor, and dug inside the middle drawer of the cherrywood buffet. She plopped back into her chair, with a calculator, pen, and paper laid out in front of her.

"For three months," she said, scribbling on the notepad, "with the insulin shots, weekly blood-sugar testing, and prescription food, plus the four hundred forty dollars already sitting on the credit card from his initial tests . . ."

The faster her pen raced across the page, the faster my heart raced.

Mom slapped the pen onto the table. "We need at least two thousand dollars."

My heart sunk down to my toes and leaked all over the rug. That was way, way more than my allowance.

I took a deep breath and lengthened my back.

"What if," I said, "instead of my birthday and Christmas presents, the money could go toward Fig's treatment? Even the money from Gran. For the next three years."

Mom and Dad traded glances.

"I don't need any new school clothes," I said. "And forget about replacing my phone or getting me a tablet."

"Maybe," Dad said, his voice growing hopeful, "I could give up cable for a year."

My stance faltered. The world must be spinning off its axis. "No Marlins? No Magic?"

Dad gave a slight shrug.

"Okay," Mom sighed. "I can give up my morning latte and afternoon sugar fix. And maybe we could even ask Gran for an extra loan, but . . ." She went back to work, making calculations on her notepad, her face scrunching into all kinds of twists, strains, and contortions.

"But we can't keep asking Gran for money. And these cutbacks aren't enough. We're still short a thousand dollars."

"Leave it to me," I said firmly. "I'll raise the rest."

Mom nodded okay, but her face grew sad. "Mira, we're really proud of you for wanting to help Fig, but you need to understand that it won't be easy to raise this kind of money."

"I understand," I said, "but I have to try."

"And even if you do raise enough," Dad added, "there's no guarantee that Fig Newton will get any better."

"But maybe he will," I insisted.

"We'll give it a try." Dad ran his palm over his messy 'fro. "But once the month is up, if the money situation doesn't change . . ."

"Then we'll have to go back to the original plan," Mom said, "and find Fig a new home."

18

SOUR LEMONS

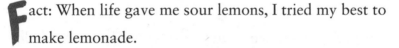

Fact: When life gave me sour lemons, I tried my best to make lemonade.

Mom had said raising $1,000 in a month wouldn't be easy, but losing Sir Fig Newton would be way harder. So first thing in the morning, I approached Mrs. B, hoping to hit her up for a lucrative babysitting gig. Since she already knew about our family situation, she'd understand the pressure I was under to get money in the bank super quick.

"I guess I could use some help to keep an eye on Sabrina," she said, her three-month-old drooling machine wriggling in a baby wrap against her chest. "You know, to get stuff done around the house."

I accepted with a firm handshake, then ran home. Operation Save Sir Fig Newton was in motion. Hypothesis: If I raised enough money to pay for his treatment, then Fig could stay at home, where he belonged. Time to test it out.

Sitting at my desk, I removed the stopper from the base of my Einstein-in-a-lab-coat piggy bank. Coins clanked onto the hard surface, followed by folded bills gliding in for a soft landing. A total of $19.26. Fifteen from my summer allowance, the rest leftover birthday money from Gran. $980.74 to go.

I grabbed a notepad and calculator. My pen scribbled across the page: $5 an hour, for three hours, three days a week. I punched the numbers into the calculator: $45 a week. Babysitting would barely add chump change to my near-zero balance. My stomach clenched. How would I ever raise enough money in just one month?

It was the middle of day one of Operation Save Fig, and my stress levels had gone from jittery subatomic particles to earth-quaking macrocosmic proportions.

Something tapped against my arm, followed by a determined "Maow. Maow?" Fully stretched on his hind legs, Fig was pawing for attention. Once I looked over, he plopped back onto the carpet into a regal sitting position, his lime-green eyes piercing into mine.

"Okay, okay." I laughed. "Time for lunch."

I headed to the kitchen. Fig trotted at my heels, his gray fur tickling my ankle. With a heavy sigh I refilled his empty water bowl. I placed his food dish at the end of the obstacle course I'd constructed the day Fig was at the vet. He gazed longingly at the food bowl and then turned to me with desperation and a hint of resentment.

"You know the deal." I shrugged. "Got to do all we can to combat this cat killer until I've raised enough money."

With an irritated switch of his tail, he spun around and slunk over to the narrow kitchen table. He stared at me, his gaze boiling. At any second the hairs around his eyes would singe. I didn't budge, only giving him a silent look of, *Bring it.*

Fig leapt onto the padded chair and onto the table-top, then skidded across the wood and into the tunnel. The polyester crinkled with each step as he worked his way through the tube. The structure wound down into the opposite chair, then onto the floor, emptying at the base of a three-level cat tower, otherwise barricaded from Fig's access. His overweight body struggled in slow motion to the second level, paused, and then lugged itself onto the top.

Fig nibbled a few dry bits but left most of the bowl's contents behind. He looked up at me, his gaze once again piercing into mine. His face clearly read: *Now* you *bring it*.

I shook off my defeatist attitude and gave Fig a confident nod, followed by a scratch under his chin. Babysitting might not be enough, but I wasn't about to give up. I was persistent.

We returned to my room, and Fig retreated onto my bed. He circled once, paused, and then plopped down into a snoring ball. I got back to work at my desk. As I tapped my pen against a notepad, my brain started to babble-storm ideas. If Einstein could use a *Gedankenexperiment*—an investigation completely worked out in his imagination—to figure out the theory of special relativity, then I could do the same to come up with a plan to save Fig.

One by one, thought bubbles trickled from my brain and out my ears, rising into the ether. Tutor. Garage sale. Yard work. Dog walker. Maid for a day. Each idea floated in front of me as I considered it.

Since it was summer, no one would need science lessons—POP. Mom was not a fan of strangers snooping through our stuff—POP. Dad would never in a million years let me use his riding lawn mower—POP. Only two dogs lived in my neighborhood: Mitzy, who always rode shotgun in Mrs. Hathaway's purse, and a Saint Bernard who was sweet but grossed me out with his constant globs of slobber. And I absolutely, positively *hated* cleaning—POP. POP.

Too bad I wasn't old enough to gamble. The lady on the six p.m. news had said the lottery prize was up to $137 million. Winning would not only mean that Sir Fig Newton would be taken care of for life, but Dad could stop the job hunt and Mom could quit her job. I could replace my dead phone, buy a tablet, and finally get that new astronomical refractor telescope, the one with the large field lens and high magnification, all at the top of my "What I Want More Than Anything Else" list—after saving Fig, of course.

But the facts were stacked against me. There's a greater chance of being struck by lightning or attacked by a shark. The odds of winning the lottery were one in three hundred million.

I wandered out of my room and headed for the kitchen. Maybe some of Tamika's *magic elixir* could revive my dwindling imagination. As I poured OJ into a glass, my ears tuned in to my parents' escalating conversation. They were crouched over the dreaded dining table, and their words were getting heated.

"The car's still making funny noises, despite your handiwork," Mom said. Dad had just fiddled under the hood the other week.

"What kind of noises? Is it a 'tick-tick-tick' sound or heavy knocking?" Dad asked.

"No tick, no knock. Nothing like that," Mom said.

"How about a pink or ping? A thud or thump? A metallic screech or scrape?"

"No, no, no." Mom sighed. "It's a high-pitched squeal, you know, like a pig."

"Hmm. When does it happen? When accelerating? Braking?"

"I don't know. Whenever I drive the stupid lemon."

Wait . . . lemon! That's it!

I'd seen kids setting up lemonade stands last summer, and for way-less-worthy causes. All I needed were some lemons and a place to set up shop, and the money was sure to pour in. I eagerly dug through the cabinets, pulling out a bag of sugar, a measuring cup, two pitchers, plastic cups, and a wooden spoon. This could work.

"You know we can't afford a mechanic." Dad's voice peaked. "Not now with Fig Newton's situation."

The tips of my ears went hot.

"Honey, we can't afford to *not* fix the car," Mom said.

"All right, you can use my truck while I work on your car."

"You know I hate that old thing." Even though I couldn't see Mom's face, I was sure it was a smashed-up expression of irritated-sourness. "Plus, I'm horrible at driving a stick."

Dad sighed. "Fine, fine. I'll take a look again this weekend."

I rushed back to my room, skirting past my parents and their ever-growing dark matter, and got to work on mapping out a plan. Fig and I couldn't afford for this lemonade stand to fail.

✫✫ 19 ✫✫

SPECIAL PRIZE INSIDE

The following morning while I watched the always wailing and wriggling Sabrina, Dad dug through the cluttered mess in the garage and found the old card table and checkered tablecloth to be my snazzy lemonade stand. I spent the afternoon painting a poster board with enticing slogans: LIQUID SUNSHINE IN A CUP; COOL & REFRESHING; SPECIAL PRIZE INSIDE.

Later that evening Dad and I went to the grocery store and stocked up on several bags of lemons and my secret sour ingredient, Lemonhead candy. I emptied the contents of my backpack onto my bed at home, making plenty of space in the bag for my guaranteed earnings.

Saturday before lunch Dad transported my stand, along with a cooler packed with ice and two large jugs of freshly made lemonade, in his used pickup truck to the small park at the front of our neighborhood. Moms pushing strollers hustled around the paved track. Families picnicked. Kids zipped and zoomed around the playground, bouncing from swings to slides to the rope-climbing structure.

I looked around and nodded in approval. The weather was on my side. The near-100-degree air sat still, heavy with moisture. Not one cloud interrupted a solid blue sky. They were the perfect elements for causing a dire need for hydration. Not even five minutes had passed when I received my first customer.

A young kid stretched onto the toes of his Air Jordans, holding out four quarters. Sweat trickled from under his baseball cap, cutting a path through crusted dirt on the side of his face.

"What's the special prize inside?" he asked.

"If I told you, then I'd spoil the surprise." I winked.

I filled a red plastic cup with lemonade and then plopped in one Lemonhead candy for an added punch of lemony goodness. I handed the kid the cup, and he downed the drink in one gulp. His eyes lit up like fireworks.

"Yum. Gimme another."

I held out my open palm. "One dollar."

The kid took off running. "Mom! I need more money."

Just as I'd hoped, the added power of sour caused a buzz. The kid came back, along with two of his friends. Within a millisecond, there was a line at least a mile long. At a dollar a glass, I racked up over twenty bucks in the first hour. By the time Dad came back to help pack up shop and go home, I'd sold over my goal of forty cups. Not one drop was left in the two plastic pitchers. Operation Save Sir Fig Newton was picking up momentum, approaching the speed of light.

The next day I set up shop again. It was so hot and steamy out that a line started to form immediately, winding like a DNA double helix. Pour, plop, take dollar, repeat. My heart soared. At this rate I would definitely make my goal by the end of the month.

Suddenly a high-pitched "Stop!" disturbed my zealous rhythm. I squinted, holding my hand to shield my eyes from the sun's glare. My eyes widened. Zooming past would-be customers, a mother dragging a young kid by the wrist shot toward my stand. A figure in khaki wearing a fluorescent vest trailed behind with a steady stride.

Shoving a plastic cup under my nose, the mother launched her tirade. "What's the meaning of this?"

Her poor kid cowered at her side, pulling down the bill of his baseball cap, his dirt-covered cheeks flaming. It was the same kid from yesterday. My very first customer.

"Are you trying to kill my son?"

The hovering mass—my former spiraling line of eager patrons—gasped.

"What? No." I shrank back. "I'm just selling lemonade. To save my cat, Sir Fig Newton."

"With hard candy?" she shrieked. She shook the cup, and the Lemonhead candy rattled inside.

"All right," the man in khaki said, maneuvering between us. My lips trembled as I silently read the patch on his button-down: PARK MAINTENANCE. "Calm down, ma'am."

"I will not calm down." She huffed. "My son here could've easily choked to death, downing her . . . her . . . *sour death-ade*!" She slammed the cup onto the stand, and the yellow candy bounced out of the cup, rolled across the tabletop, and nose-dived onto the grass.

Shocked commentary erupted among the crowd.

"I-I . . ." Stunned, my voice plummeted. "I wasn't trying to hurt anybody."

"I know you didn't mean any harm, miss," the park worker said. "Do you have a permit for this stand?"

I shook my head.

"Then, unfortunately, you'll have to close up shop until you do." His eyes were apologetic, but his tone was firm.

The mother gave me one last death-stare before pulling her son out of the park.

I felt absolutely, positively, 100 percent awful. I couldn't believe I hadn't really thought about a hard candy maybe being dangerous. What if her kid *had* gotten hurt? The thought made my entire body shudder. I stood there, numb, watching everyone—and my Operation Save Fig funds—stroll away. I should've known better, but there was nothing I could do now. So

I packed up my stand and waited over an hour for my dad to pick me up.

The whole ride home, I whined about my disastrous day.

"Can you believe it? A hundred and fifty dollars for a permit! I'm so mad at myself." I huffed. "Because I didn't take the time to research and think everything through, Operation Save Sir Fig Newton is on life support. How am I going to raise enough money now?"

"You'll think of something," Dad said distractedly, pulling into our driveway.

But no matter how hard I focused, struggling to come up with a new plan of attack, my mind drew a blank. Even a glass of OJ didn't help.

That evening the sky darkened and thick sheets of rain blanketed our small town. Fig camped out under my bed, while I sulked, sitting on top. The family computer was balanced on my lap. With all my attention on Operation Save Fig, I realized that I'd never emailed Thomas about Fig's official diagnosis.

Just as I was about to reply to his last email, I noticed that Thomas was online. I sent him a link to join me on a video call. Within seconds Thomas's narrow face, peeking out from under his curly shag, popped onto the screen.

"Miranium!"

"Hey," I said with a weak smile.

Thomas frowned. "What's wrong?"

"Everything."

I saw my face on the screen crumple in despair. My eyes darted to my lap. I shared everything that had happened since we'd last talked five days ago. From my parents' awful plan to give up Sir Fig Newton for adoption, to my epic fail with the lemonade stand.

"I don't know what I'm going to do. And now I have STEM Girls camp all week, so I'll have even less time to raise enough money." My hand swiped across my eyes to make sure no tears escaped.

Thomas's forehead wrinkled. "I can't believe your parents were going to give away Sir Fig! Why do adults always want to split up friends?"

"Right?" I shook my head repeatedly.

"Remember when we were working on that geometry problem and neither of us could figure it out, so we played video games instead until my mom yelled at us to get back to work?"

"Yeah, and?"

"Once we sat back down, it was like the answer was staring right at you. You instantly knew how to solve it. Maybe STEM Girls is the break your brain needs. But, hey, with your stubbornness superpower, I just know you'll raise the money in time. You're Miranium! The toughest, strongest element in the whole universe."

"Yeah, I guess," I said with a sheepish grin.

We kept on talking as if there weren't a billion and one miles between us. He shared how noisy his new neighborhood was, and we laughed about the time we performed a dance routine to "Shining Star"—one of Dad's favorite oldies disco hits. We talked about basketball and whether Thomas should try out for the team at his new school. We agreed how weird it was that Tamika now lived in his old house and how sweet it would be for me to finally beat her at the next science fair.

I felt happy and sad at the same time. Sad that we wouldn't be starting school together. Sad that he was no longer right down the street. And sad that I still had no clue how I was going to raise enough money to save Fig. But just spending time with Thomas online and knowing that he believed in me truly made me feel like the strongest, luckiest element in the world.

20

STEM GIRLS JUST WANT TO HAVE FUN

Last night's thunderstorm continued to rage on into the next day. Despite the downpour and the fact that Operation Sir Fig was in crisis, I decided to take Thomas's advice and give my brain—and nerves—a break while at STEM Girls camp. High-pitched chatter greeted me as I entered the classroom at the local community college. Looming through the tall windows along the back wall, dark skies were crammed with nimbus clouds. Even with the overhead fluorescent lights the room felt dreary.

"So glad to have you back at camp, Mira."

I turned to see Mrs. Lee standing by my side, wearing the same outfit she'd worn all week last year, and the year before that—jeans, sneakers, and a silly shirt. Today's tee was reddish-purple with the words "STEM Girls Just Want to Have Fun" across the front.

"Thanks, Mrs. Lee. Happy to be back."

"Looks like you and Tamika are the only returning students." She nodded in Tamika's direction. Tamika flashed a suspiciously bright smile. "Go ahead and take a seat. We'll be starting in just a minute."

I scanned the classroom and frowned. Mrs. Lee was right. I didn't recognize any of the other girls. There were five round tables, each with four chairs. The only empty seat was between a tiny redhead with matching freckles, and my nemesis. My frown deepened.

"Are you as elated as I am?" Tamika asked, straightening her oversized flower.

I gave a slight eye roll with my nod as I slipped into the chair.

"Good morning, girls!" Mrs. Lee's voice boomed, silencing the chatter. "And welcome to STEM Girls camp. Over the next week we'll be learning about different careers in STEM, through conversations with local STEM professionals and hands-on activities. But first, since we've got girls here from all over Brevard County, let's do a fun introduction game!

"Take a quick look at the girls sitting at your table." Mrs. Lee paused, her gigantic smile somehow growing larger. "This will be your team for the week when we create our own apps."

Thunder rumbled in the distance as the heavy rains continued to beat against the classroom windows. The overhead lights flickered. I scanned every face at my table. My gaze landed last on Tamika. Oh no. My nemesis and I were being forced to work together! This week that was supposed to be a fun break for my brain had just turned into my worst nightmare.

"We'll spend the next ten minutes getting to know your neighbors. Then when time's up, you'll introduce the person on your left to the entire class. Let's begin . . . ," Mrs. Lee said, and then glanced at her watch. "Now!"

"Brilliant," Tamika said. "I get to introduce you, *El*mira."

"Mira," I huffed.

"I'm disappointed we won't be building rockets," Tamika continued. "And now we can't go to the observatory, since it's still closed because of the damage caused by Hurricane Irma. But making our own app—together—sounds prodigious."

Releasing a heavy sigh, I finally understood the theory of relativity. Spending an hour with my best friend, Thomas, video-chatting last night had seemed to fly by in a minute. But sitting here with Tamika for the past minute had been longer than any hour.

"I guess I should tell you about myself so you have something to say," I said. Tamika leaned in with eyes as wide as the fake flower behind her ear. "I knew I wanted to become an astrophysicist when I was nine. Astronomy is cool because we can ask questions about the universe, and the universe is everything that exists! It's planets and stars and black holes and galaxies. And someday I'll be—"

"Okay, everyone," Mrs. Lee said. "Time to switch neighbors."

I didn't even get enough time to talk about becoming an astronaut and walking on Mars, or my favorite experiments or my best furry friend, Sir Fig. Oh well, at least I no longer had to stare at Tamika's annoyingly smug grin.

I turned to face the tiny redhead on my left. She slouched in her chair like she was trying to disappear. "Hi. I'm Mira."

Avoiding eye contact, she barely fluttered her hand. I guessed that was her attempt at saying hello.

"What's your name?" I asked.

Her gaze still glued to her lap, she mumbled something that sounded like "poppa" or "puppy," but that couldn't be right. She mumbled again, and this time it clicked.

"Poppy!" I said.

She finally looked at me, nodding eagerly.

"Do you like science?"

Poppy shrugged.

"Coding?"

Her head bounced up and down so hard, I'd thought the grin on her face might fall off.

"Time's up," Mrs. Lee said. "Okay, you each get a minute to introduce your new friend to the rest of the group."

Almost twenty minutes had passed when Mrs. Lee finally called on our table. Poppy went first. Her face hot pink, she somehow managed to actually speak.

"Becky," she said, waving at the girl next to her. Becky's round face was pink too, but I was pretty sure it was from too much sun. "Loves animals. Two brothers."

A few girls giggled, but I turned to Poppy and gave her a reassuring smile.

"This is my new friend, Tamika," Becky said. She flung back her long black hair, bringing attention to her sparkly earrings. "She loves science, especially everything to do with space. She's a huge *Star Trek* fan and wants to be a pilot someday, just like her uncle."

Huh. I'd never known that Tamika wanted to fly a plane. That would be pretty cool.

"This is my friend, *El*mira. We go to the same school, and she's the only person who has ever come close to beating me at the science fair. She's really smart, and after seeing her experiments on moon phases and black holes, I know she'll definitely make a stellar astrophysicist someday."

My face grew warm. I wasn't sure if I was irritated or flattered. I guess a bit of both.

The rest of the day flew by. We made catapults out of

Popsicle sticks, rubber bands, and a plastic spoon. Then we took turns launching fuzzy pom-poms to see whose went the farthest. Later a botanist and member of the Florida Native Plant Society spoke to us about why native plants are so important. We learned that wildlife, like deer and butterflies, depend on native plants for survival, and if we remove the bushes and small trees along our coastlines, then hurricanes could cause increased coastal erosion.

The next day at camp, the rain slowed to a drizzle. Mrs. Lee floated around the room checking in on the teams as we started on our app project, her shirt boasting the words "Back in My Day, We Had Nine Planets."

After we unanimously chose Becky's suggested team name, "Apptitude," we brainstormed what kind of app we wanted to build, one that would help solve a problem.

"How about a game that helps you learn Spanish?" Becky said. "Users can choose their location, like a restaurant or school, and then click on different objects to see and hear the words in Spanish."

"Or a homework tracker," Tamika said, "where you enter all your assignments, the steps to complete them, and due dates, and then mark them off when finished."

"A mood-music app," I added, "where you can find a song to match or help change your current mood."

Becky, Tamika, and I continued to share ideas popcorn-style as Poppy diligently wrote them down: a star identifier, a personality quiz to see which character from *The Baby-Sitters Club* you're most like, and a dream analyzer.

Suddenly Poppy laid down her pen and softly said, "Find fun and friends."

We all stared at her, wide-eyed.

"An app to find things to do in your area, like STEM Girls camp, and maybe even make some new friends," her voice squeaked.

The three of us locked gazes. "Yes!" we cried in unison.

Poppy's pink cheeks inflated as she smiled.

We got busy working on our paper prototypes. Picking up a blank sheet of paper, I said, "Let's start with the logo."

Everyone pitched in, including Poppy, and after some debate we settled on our app name and logo. We decided on "*F* cubed"—which stood for "Finding Fun and Friends"—with a white capital *F* and a white superscript three on an orange background. Using the pile of construction paper, markers, and tape, we began sketching screenshots of how we imagined our app would look, on cardboard cutouts shaped like cell phones.

Becky started to giggle. "What if people think that the three *F*s stand for 'fee-fi-fo'?"

Tamika shook her head. "Not plausible. It's 'fee-fi-fo-*fum*.'"

"That's just it," Becky said, laughing harder. "Maybe they'll think we forgot the 'fum.'"

Poppy and I started to giggle.

"Or how about, 'fiddle-faddle-fuddle,'" I chimed in.

Becky busted up laughing, and then we all joined in, even Tamika.

"Well, looks like you girls are having a good time," Mrs. Lee said as she approached our table. This just made us laugh harder.

I had figured camp would be good, but I'd never expected to actually be Finding Fun and Friends, like our proposed app. Especially with having to work with Tamika. The week zoomed by. We kept working on our project, finishing up our paper prototypes and playing around with some app-building software. Poppy was a coding wizard, completing several of the app screens, including one that featured a dancing mascot named Friendly the Giraffe.

And Mrs. Lee's T-shirt selection continued to never disappoint. On Wednesday her shirt had a cat playing with a ball of yarn with the words "String Theory" underneath. On Thursday her shirt read BLACK HOLES ARE OUT OF SIGHT.

In between building apps, we continued to try different STEM activities. Using borax, water, and pipe cleaners, we made our own crystals. We also went to the computer lab, where we learned about 3D printing, including that the queen's costume in the movie *Black Panther* was mostly 3D printed! Together with the computer science teacher, we designed a key chain that said STEM GIRLS next to a raised star. The teacher promised to print a key chain for each of us to take home before the week ended.

Probably my favorite thing, other than joking around with my team, was when an astrophysics grad student from the University of Central Florida came to speak. Not only did Ayana work in planetary science, but she also had really cool hair braided in a complicated pattern with beads on the ends. She used telescopes to study near-Earth asteroids—those close enough to the edge of the asteroid belt that they could escape and come toward Earth!

"How many of you have heard of Galileo?" Ayana asked. "Or Neil deGrasse Tyson?"

Almost everyone raised their hand.

"What about Dr. Vera Cooper Rubin?"

Only a few hands remained in the air.

"She's the astrophysicist who confirmed the existence of dark matter," I said, "the invisible stuff that makes up the universe."

Ayana nodded. "And has anyone ever heard of Dr. Beth A. Brown?"

The room fell silent. Not one hand rose.

"She was the first Black woman to earn a doctorate in astronomy from the University of Michigan, and she's the reason I decided to pursue a career in astronomy," Ayana said, fiddling with her braids. "My physics teacher in high school told me that going into astrophysics would be too hard for someone like me. But when I saw that Dr. Brown had worked at NASA, collecting data on elliptical galaxies and black holes, I knew I could do it too."

Whoa. I'd never known there were Black female astronomers!

"I encourage all of you to find a mentor. Check out library books, research online, and keep attending classes like this one. It doesn't matter if it's someone you know personally or someone from a hundred years ago. Role models are an important reminder that even though there aren't as many women today working in STEM as men, they do exist, and one day you can be a role model for someone just like yourself!"

I thought about my neighbor Mrs. B. Not just because she was an aerospace engineer at NASA but also because she was best friends with her sister, and she was a mom, a wife, and a good friend to me.

Then there were all the awesome astronauts—Sally Ride, Mae Jemison, and Ellen Ochoa—and amazing astronomers—Dr. Rubin, Dr. Brown, and soon-to-be Dr. Ayana. I had a ton of role models, and after I walked on Mars or discovered Planet Nine, then I would be someone's hero too.

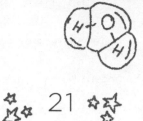

21

REBOOT AND START OVER

Fact: Just like the Fourth of July fireworks, I was bursting with energy. My thoughts no longer bounced around, imagining the worst. I was finally having fun. Thomas was right. STEM Girls was the time-out that my brain needed.

The night before the last day of camp, I sat on my bed with the family computer balanced in my lap. Sir Fig Newton lay by my side in a tight ball, wheezing softly. Humming an upbeat tune, I got online and started to go through my latest email thread with Thomas.

From: Thomas Thompson

To: Mira Williams

Date: Jul 2, 2:38 PM

Subject: How's Camp?

Hey! I tried calling, but you were still at camp. How's it going? Feeling better yet? Like I said, you're Miranium, the strongest element ever. Nothing can stop you!

Nothing exciting here. I tried to convince my parents to go to the Fourth of July fireworks on the National Mall, but my mom said we could just watch it on TV. At least I get to choose what we order for takeout.

Give Sir Fig Newton a nose boop from me.

Write back soon,

Thomas

P.S. How does a scientist freshen her breath? (Wait . . . for . . . it. . . . With experi-mints!)

From: Mira Williams

To: Thomas Thompson

Date: Jul 2, 7:38 PM

Subject: RE: How's Camp?

Hey! STEM Girls is going great, even with Tamika and me on the same team. Yup, you read that right. Tamika and I are working together and we're actually having fun! Shocking, right?

On Friday our team has to present our app idea, and every member has to speak. You know I don't really like giving speeches, but it shouldn't be bad since we're doing it as a group. This really shy girl, Poppy, came up with our app. It's called "Finding Fun & Friends." That would be neat if we could finish it and you could use it to find fun things to do in DC that your parents would take you to.

Once camp has ended, hopefully my brain will be supercharged enough to come up with a plan to raise more than enough money for Fig.

Best friends forever,

Mira

From: Thomas Thompson

To: Mira Williams

Date: Jul 3, 8:05 PM

Subject: RE: How's Camp?

Awesome news alert: I met this really cool guy Pete at the local pool. We're both PlayStation masters. He knows cheat codes I've never seen before. And just like us, he's a huge *Doctor Who* fan.

We went to the National Museum of American History today. It was better than Disney. Did you know that the original Star-Spangled Banner weighs 50 pounds? That's just one of more than 1.8 million artifacts at the museum!

And my parents said it was okay for me to go with Pete and his family to see the national fireworks tomorrow. I bet it'll be a blast LOL.

Maybe you can come visit soon. You'd love Pete. We could all go see the Einstein Memorial. I guess DC isn't so bad after all.

Thomas

Awesome news? Really cool guy? My blissful energy fizzled. I was glad that Thomas sounded happy, but it really hurt to know he was so happy hanging out with someone other than me. Maybe I'd made him jealous when I'd said that Tamika and I were actually having fun. But he knew that she'd forever be my nemesis.

I hit the reply button and started to type.

From: Mira Williams

To: Thomas Thompson

Date: Jul 4, 6:46 PM

Subject: RE: How's Camp?

Hey.

I froze, my hands hovering over the keyboard. The blank space on the screen stretched taller and wider, into infinity. My atoms were packed so tightly together, I had no energy to move. Thomas was all good without me.

Closing the laptop, I decided that I'd write him back later. I shook my head, hoping to shake away the tense jitters. Gently stroking Fig's gray coat, I whispered, "It's all good."

* * * * * *

It was the last day of STEM Girls camp, and each team was bustling around, getting ready to present their app idea to the class. Sunshine streamed in through the windows along the back wall, but I was far from feeling sunny. I'd barely gotten any sleep the night before because I hadn't been able to stop thinking about how much fun Thomas was probably having with Pete at the Fourth of July fireworks. I was too tired now to even chuckle at Mrs. Lee's shirt—navy blue with a bunch of otters wearing space helmets, floating in a star-filled sky with the words "Otter Space" underneath.

"First up," Mrs. Lee said, "Team Planet Earth."

Four girls from the back table dashed to the front of the room and presented their app game about an alien landing on Earth. The user had to get the alien back to its home planet by passing a quiz. Each true-or-false question taught the user—and the alien—basic Earth science facts. Even though it was a cool idea, I had a hard time paying attention. Slumped in my chair, my head propped up by my hands, I had to muster every ounce of energy to keep from yawning.

One by one each team presented their app idea, and once finished, they received a standing ovation. Team Coding Queens had designed an app that predicted the future. Team Tech Wizards had thought of an app that taught different dance moves, while Team Girls Save the World had created a save-the-sea-turtles game.

"And now our final team," Mrs. Lee said. "Team Apptitude."

My teammates bounced up to the front of the room, with me trudging behind.

"We are Becky, Poppy, *El*mira, and Tamika," Tamika said, waving at each of us as she called out our names, "and we are Team Apptitude! Today we're going to tell you all about our app, Finding Fun and Friends. It's perfect for when you're on vacation, all your friends are away for the summer, or you just moved to a new town and you're bored and looking for something fun to do."

Frowning, I instantly thought about Thomas and how he must have felt moving to a strange new city. With a heavy sigh I held up one of the cardboard cutouts shaped like a cell phone. It detailed our app's home screen. At the top was our logo F^3 with the words "Are you ready to Find Fun & Friends?" Below was a drop-down box to select your zip code, followed by a checkbox list of various activities, like sports, concerts, and volunteering.

"Once you give your location and choose some of your favorite things," I said, "the app will figure out . . ."

My mouth froze along with my brain. I just kept picturing Thomas using the app and checking off American history, video games, and basketball. And once he hit the go button, he'd get the result: *Hang out with Pete*.

"Mira," Poppy whispered.

I felt a nudge against my shoulder, but my brain continued to malfunction. "Umm, the app will, umm . . ." I desperately wished I could reboot and start over.

Before I had a chance to recover, Tamika jumped in. "The app will figure out what activities are happening nearby that you might be interested in and will give you a list of options."

My cheeks burned. How could Tamika embarrass me like that? I would've eventually remembered the rest of my speech. I felt humiliated. I didn't even hear Becky or Poppy speak. I was trapped in a black hole, stuck in a soundproof bubble sealed away from the rest of the universe. It wasn't until the class erupted in applause that the sound barrier was broken.

The rest of our last class together was spent eating pizza and cake and sharing our favorite moments from the week. I sat at one of the back tables, picking at the pepperoni on my slice. I didn't feel like sharing or laughing or pretending that everything was all good. I just wanted to go home.

"Mira," said a soft voice.

I yanked my head up, ready to tell whoever it was to leave me alone. My face softened once I realized it was Poppy. She stood there, rocking on her heels. "It's our last day together," she finally managed with a small frown.

"Yeah," I said.

"I know what it's like . . . when you can't find the words," she said, "but that was really nice of Tamika to help you out. It's nice when someone has your back."

Humph. I doubted that. What about when she'd said we can't all win first place? When she'd finished my speech just now, she'd been trying to show me up like she always did at the science fair. But as the day wound down and Poppy's words really sank in, I wondered. Maybe Tamika hadn't been trying to take over the presentation to embarrass me.

Maybe she really did have my back. Just like Thomas always did.

22

NEVER CONSULT WITH THE ENEMY

Thunderstorms raged for several days after STEM Girls camp, and I was trapped indoors for what felt like forever. When I finally got to go outside, it felt totally new. The lawn, still soaked in pools of mud from the storms, looked like the Florida Everglades. At least the heat had less bite and the humidity had dropped to tolerable levels, so I was able to hang out on the sidewalk and think about all my predicaments.

I still hadn't emailed Thomas back, even though he'd emailed me again. Twice. Apparently he'd had a great time watching the national fireworks with his new friend, Pete. And now Pete was teaching Thomas how to play basketball. That was *my* thing! When Thomas had called yesterday for our weekly chat, I'd lied and told my dad that I wasn't feeling well and to tell Thomas that we'd catch up next week. Technically it wasn't a total lie. My stomach kind of hurt because I felt horrible that things were changing so fast between us.

My head drooped.

And even worse, my Einstein piggy bank held only $158.26. The rain might have stopped, but my worry about how to save Sir Fig Newton hadn't. If it weren't for my babysitting gig, I wouldn't have been making any money at all.

Einstein once said, "Logic will get you from A to B. Imagination will take you everywhere." At STEM Girls camp, I'd had so much fun brainstorming app ideas with my fellow teammates. But ever since I'd messed up our presentation, my mind still wasn't cooperating. With only two weeks left to raise money for Operation Save Fig, I had no clue how I was going to do it.

Inhaling deeply, I forced my chin up. No time for moping. There was nothing I could do about Thomas right now. More important, Operation Save Sir Fig Newton needed my full attention.

My fingers rubbed over the raised star on the STEM Girls key chain in my pocket. Too bad Team Apptitude wasn't there to help me come up with a plan. Fellow scientists who could analyze the facts and help solve the problem. Even though our team had exchanged email addresses during camp, Dad was hogging the laptop for his job search. I needed help right now.

Poppy lived over the bridge and near the mall in a nearby town, which was fifteen minutes away by car. Becky was even farther away near the beach. Even if I knew their home addresses, I could never get there by bike.

I really needed someone who matched my caliber, and though obviously nobody was as good a scientist as me, if only I could find someone close . . .

I slapped my hand to my forehead. There *was* a fellow scientist in my hood. And she lived at the end of my block. I knew I shouldn't. I wouldn't be able to bear the smug look on her face if I went to her for help. But . . .

As much as I hated to admit it, I could really use

Tamika's brainpower. Sure, the last time I'd seen the enemy, she'd made me look ridiculous by jumping in and finishing my part of our team presentation. But Poppy had said that she'd done it because she had my back. Could I really trust Tamika? I wasn't sure what to think.

With clenched fists, I straightened my stance. I still didn't like it, but winning means never giving up. I heaved a deep sigh and forced myself to march down to the end of the street.

I stood on the familiar front porch, surrounded by foreign wicker furniture. My hand heavy, I knocked on the red front door and waited. I peeked over each shoulder, debating a last-second escape. Dread gnawed at my gut. To top it off, I was still having trouble accepting that Thomas no longer lived there. I half expected his wide eyes to peep around the door to check who it was. My shoulders sank when Mrs. Smith answered.

"Well, hello. It's Mira, right?"

I nodded. "Is Tamika here?"

"Come on in." Mrs. Smith smiled, opening the door wide.

Sitting on the couch, Tamika faced a stack of papers alongside a tower of envelopes on the living room table.

The early afternoon sun poured through the window, adding warmth to the stiff furniture I'd encountered two weeks ago.

Tamika's hands paused in stuffing envelopes as she raised her brows in my direction. "Flabbergasted to see you here, *El*mira."

I shook my head slowly. She was so darn weird.

Mrs. Smith seemed to think so too, rolling her eyes and giving me an apologetic look. "Is that how you greet company, T? Offer your friend a drink."

Tamika grimaced. I repressed a giggle.

Her scowl morphed into a suspicious grin. "Something to drink?"

"Sure," I said. As she headed toward the kitchen, I called after her, "Anything but lemonade."

Mrs. Smith waved for me to sit down. She picked a single page off the top of the pile and carefully folded the top a third of the way down, then the bottom of the page up.

"What you guys doing?" I asked.

Mrs. Smith stuffed the folded page inside an envelope, already addressed and stamped, and sealed it shut.

"Mailing out thank-you letters for my upcoming marathon." She held out one of the papers.

> Dear Mr. and Mrs. Hawbecker,
>
> I can't thank you enough for your generous $100 donation. Thanks to your support, I've raised almost half of my $2,000 goal for the Diabetes Action Team. Training continues to go strong for the Disney Marathon. Can you believe I'm going to run 26.2 miles?!? HA! Me neither. You know how I hate to sweat . . .

I stopped reading and handed back the letter. "People gave you *money*?"

"The goal's twelve hundred dollars, but I always ask for more. Got to go big." She picked up her laptop and turned it toward me. "This is my fundraising page."

The bold header across the top of the screen read *Disney Marathon Fundraiser to Beat Diabetes!* There was a collage of pictures underneath showcasing what looked like a heavier, darker-skinned version of my dad. He had that same huge grin that was about to break into a deep belly laugh.

"That was my brother," Mrs. Smith said with a sad smile.

"I'm sorry," I said. I thought about Mom and Grandma

Millie, and Dad losing his friend. It must be really hard losing *forever* forever someone you love.

"Thanks," Mrs. Smith said. "It's true what they say. Time heals all wounds. Or at least most of the pain."

She resumed stuffing letters, and I returned my gaze to her laptop. A list of names and their donation amount occupied the right-hand side of the screen. The donation total—*$950 raised of $2,000 goal*—was displayed at the top of the list, with a huge *DONATE NOW* button underneath. I quickly memorized the web address.

"Even though an automatic thank-you email is sent to donors," Mrs. Smith said, "it just feels more personable to take the time to send an actual letter. Feels like the least I can do."

My brain launched into overdrive.

"There are at least what, forty, fifty letters here?"

Fifty people times twenty-dollar donations each, plus the other half from Mom and Dad, would give us exactly what Sir Fig Newton needed for three months: two thousand smackeroos for insulin, food, and weekly blood-sugar tests.

Tamika nudged my shoulder with the glass of OJ.

"Eighty-one letters," she said. "Scientists are always exact."

I took the glass, and Tamika plopped back onto the couch. "So what brings you to my new abode, *El*mira?"

"Had a time-sensitive dilemma," I said, "but I managed to figure it out. Sometimes runners-up have good ideas too, you know."

Tamika eyed me suspiciously.

"So, eighty-one, huh?" I said. "I don't even know that many people."

Mrs. Smith laughed. "I thought the same thing. But then I reached out to friends and family through email and social media. Then coworkers, old classmates, and even strangers donated and spread the word. The more people you ask, the more chances some will say yes."

I leaned back into the cushions, running my finger around the glass rim. I wasn't allowed on social media until my thirteenth birthday, but I could email classmates and teachers. Einstein was right. The power to create with your mind would take you everywhere, and my imagination was blasting out of orbit. Who knew I'd find inspiration here, in enemy territory?

"Let me give you guys a hand." I set down my glass

and picked up a letter and matching envelope.

"I'd appreciate that," Mrs. Smith said. She started to hum a funky tune that sounded like something from Dad's music collection.

My head bounced along to her upbeat melody as I found my own rhythm to folding and stuffing envelopes. The three of us were like well-oiled robots, our assembly line never veering off course: fold, stuff, seal, repeat.

Neither Tamika nor I brought up our app presentation at camp, which was fine with me. I wanted to forget that awful, horrible day. After a few minutes I hummed along to Mrs. Smith's song, a smile plastered on my face. Operation Save Sir Fig Newton was back on track.

The following day, after passing Mom's "spic-and-span" room test, I sat at my desk, hunched in front of the family laptop. I carefully studied every inch of the Disney Marathon Fundraiser to Beat Diabetes website.

> My brother lost his fight against type 2 diabetes and passed away last year. My community's love and emotional support helped me and my family through our trying time and has kept my hope alive that one

day we'll put an end to this disease. Once again I
need help. On January 4, I'll be running in the Disney
World Marathon in support of the Diabetes Action
Team—a nonprofit organization committed to the
prevention and treatment of diabetes. I've committed
to completing 26.2 miles and to raising a minimum
of $2,000. Will you join me in this commitment? Just
$20, $10, even $5 could make the difference between
life and death . . .

More donors were listed, with a total of $1,050 raised.
Mrs. Smith had raised an additional hundred dollars in
less than twenty-four hours! I clicked on the collage of
pictures, and the first photo loaded, taking up the full
screen.

I scrolled through, my eyes hesitating on a picture of
Tamika with her uncle. They were standing in front of
the Orlando Science Center, her uncle pointing at his
shirt that read NEVER TRUST AN ATOM, THEY MAKE UP
EVERYTHING with the science center logo underneath.
Tamika was . . . smiling. Not one of those smarter-than-
thou smirks. She wore a real big grin and was glowing
from head to toe, as if she'd just gotten her pilot's license.

My attention turned to Sir Fig Newton napping on my made bed. His head lifted, his drowsy gaze staring me down.

"You're right, Fig. I'm the toughest, strongest, most indestructible element ever, and I've got work to do."

Mrs. Smith might have joked on her fundraising page that she didn't like to sweat, but I sure hated to run. Running a mile in PE last year had been *way* worse than having to clean my room. Huffing and puffing around the track, I'd thought I'd never catch my breath and would eventually drown in my own sweat. But I *did* love to ride my bike.

Mrs. Smith's website also talked about all the fun spots where friends and family could cheer her on during the race, like Cinderella's castle at Magic Kingdom, the Spaceship Earth geosphere at Epcot, or the Tree of Life at Animal Kingdom.

That got me thinking. Why not bike around town instead? I could ride past all my favorite places, like the library and doughnut shop. Twenty-six point two miles was more than my legs could handle, but I could easily bike about five miles.

I took one last look at Mrs. Smith's website and clicked on the *Start a Fundraising Page* link at the top of the screen. An online form popped up, and I entered my name and email address. The mouse cursor was hovering over the *NEXT* button when I noticed small print underneath.

> By continuing, you agree to our terms and accept our privacy policy. With or without registering, if you are under 18 years of age, you must be at least 13 years old *and* have your parent's or guardian's permission to create an account. If you are under 13 years of age, you are *not* authorized to use this website.

Holding my head in my hands, I squeezed my eyes shut. Why should I be punished just because I wasn't a teenager yet? That was so unfair! I should've known better. Never consult with the enemy.

23

GOT TO GO BIG

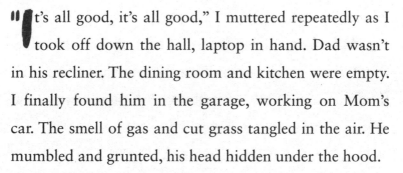

"It's all good, it's all good," I muttered repeatedly as I took off down the hall, laptop in hand. Dad wasn't in his recliner. The dining room and kitchen were empty. I finally found him in the garage, working on Mom's car. The smell of gas and cut grass tangled in the air. He mumbled and grunted, his head hidden under the hood.

I continued chanting under my breath.

Dad's head popped up. He glanced at the laptop in my tight grip. "All good, Mira?"

"No!" I stomped my foot. "It's *not* all good!"

Dad set down his wrench and wiped his hands on a stained rag. He led me back into the house, to the dreaded dining room table, and waved for me to sit down. I shook my head, my nerves too itchy to stay still.

"What's wrong, Mira girl?"

I handed him the closed laptop. He lifted the top, and the *Start a Fundraising Page* with my name and email address loaded onto the screen.

Dad furrowed his brow. "What's this?"

"This is how I'm supposed to save Sir Fig Newton." Shaking, I pointed at the small print at the bottom of the page. "But the stupid site says I'm too young to raise money."

Dad heaved a sigh. He tapped his finger on the table-top. "I know this isn't easy. First the lemonade stand, now this." He waved his hand at the screen. "But I'm so proud of you, fighting for Fig Newton."

I could tell that Dad hated how much I hurt, and that he wanted to make everything all normal again. His words hanging in the air brought no comfort.

"But I'm losing the fight."

The longer Dad stared at me, struggling with how to

respond, the more my tough exterior withered. I desperately wanted to live up to my nickname, Miranium. But how could I keep strong with hurricane-force winds constantly trying to tear me down?

"You know," Dad said, closing the laptop, "when I was your age, we had a fundraiser for Little League. Most of my teammates' parents sold their candy for them, to coworkers, friends, or they just bought the whole box themselves. Your Gran said that since it was for my team, it was my responsibility. So I went door-to-door, begging neighbors to buy candy bars."

"How'd it go?"

"I sold every last one." Dad grinned. He poked me in the gut. "Sometimes when you think you've done all you can, you have to dig down deep and find that extra oomph that helps you get through what seems like an impossible situation."

With every test of my theory—if I raise enough money to pay for Fig's treatment, then he'll get to stay home— each attempt had failed. Some believed that Einstein once said, "Learn from yesterday, live for today, hope for tomorrow." A new plan started to form.

The weight on my shoulders lessened. Instead of fund-raising online, I could go door-to-door. That just might work! It had to, not only for Sir Fig Newton but for me.

The next day, I stood on Thomas's old front porch, grip-ping a bunch of flyers. Even though Thomas was a light-year, or about six trillion and one miles away, somehow it just felt right to start my fundraising here. I glanced at the large tree across the street. The sun glared, the air hot and the world hazy. I took a deep breath, my back stretching tall like a live oak. With one more heavy exhale, I rang the doorbell.

"Hi, Mrs. Smith."

"Mira, been seeing a lot of you lately," she replied with a smile as big as her natural fluffy hair.

Mrs. Smith turned her head and started to call out, "Tami—"

"No!" I said a little too loudly, waving my arms. "I'm here to see you."

Too late. Tamika came bounding down the hall. Once she saw me, her mouth broke out into that evil scientist's grin.

"Can't get enough of me, huh?"

I ignored the enemy and handed Mrs. Smith my flyer.

I'd stayed up all night making it. To reel in the attention of animal lovers, there was the cutest photo of Sir Fig Newton from when he was a kitten batting at a ball. The words **"there is no cure"** and **"diabetes"** and **"you can help"** were all in bold. And there was a blurb about my commitment to riding my bike six miles throughout my hometown to raise $1,000 for Sir Fig Newton, making stops at Kennedy Middle School, the library, the supposedly haunted Ashley's Restaurant, and Entenmann's Outlet Bakery. All the major landmarks.

Dad had taken me to the library in the morning to use the copier, and we'd had two hundred fifty copies made. He'd even agreed to a few extra days beyond my one-month deadline so that the bike-a-thon fell on the last Sunday in July. My bank balance was down to $133.26, with each copy costing a dime, but like Mrs. Smith had said, got to go big.

Tamika leaned around her mother, spying at the flyer.

"Operation Save Sir Fig Newton?" She furrowed her brow. "You stole this from my mom."

"I didn't *steal* it," I answered impatiently. "I'm a scientist. I did some research and applied my findings."

"How long has your cat been sick?" Mrs. Smith asked, leaning against the door with folded arms. My face winced at her clanking bangles. I couldn't tell if this was an interrogation or if she was actually concerned.

"I'd hypothesized it for a while, and the vet proved my theory two weeks ago," I said. "But Fig's treatment is too expensive for my parents, so I talked them into letting me help raise money. So here I am."

"But cats can't get diabetes," Tamika huffed. "That's a people's disease, right, Mom?"

"He is *too* sick." My cheeks flamed. "Call my dad. Or the vet. They'll tell you. Fig has the silent cat killer." I gave Tamika my laser eyes. "And he'll die if I don't save him."

"No need for any calls." Mrs. Smith unfolded her arms. "Tamika, go get my purse."

Tamika rolled her eyes at me. "Gosh, *El*mira, you're so melodra—"

"My purse." Mrs. Smith cut Tamika off in that tone you knew not to argue with.

Tamika slipped away down the hall in silence.

"You must really love him," Mrs. Smith said with a warm smile.

"He's family."

"And there's nothing we wouldn't do for family, isn't that right?"

I nodded.

Tamika returned, glaring in my direction. She handed her mother an oversized tan bag covered in capital Cs all facing different directions. Mrs. Smith dug out her wallet, her bracelets jingling, and then handed me a fifty-dollar bill. Tamika's jaw dropped, probably as wide as my eyes were popping. For once my nemesis was at a loss for words.

"Oh. My. Einstein," I whispered as I gingerly took the bill. "Thanks so much." Excitement buzzed in my chest. "And Fig thanks you too."

"Good luck, Mira," Mrs. Smith said.

I made my way off the porch, a skip to my strut, before Tamika could get her mom to change her mind.

"Does your cat really have diabetes?" Tamika's voice called after me.

I paused in the driveway and turned around, ready to

get into it, but then realized her words weren't in attack mode. She looked curious. Maybe even a little concerned. I remembered the photo of her and her uncle in front of the science center.

"Yeah," I called back.

"I hope you reach your goal." Without another word Tamika slipped back into her house and closed the door.

24

ALL THE BIG, STUPID BUTS

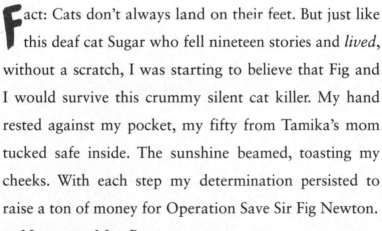

act: Cats don't always land on their feet. But just like this deaf cat Sugar who fell nineteen stories and *lived*, without a scratch, I was starting to believe that Fig and I would survive this crummy silent cat killer. My hand rested against my pocket, my fifty from Tamika's mom tucked safe inside. The sunshine beamed, toasting my cheeks. With each step my determination persisted to raise a ton of money for Operation Save Sir Fig Newton.

Next stop, Mrs. B.

"Oh, isn't this adorable!" she gushed over my flyer,

213

holding it in front of Sabrina's drooling face while making one of those ridiculous coochy-coo faces. "You are one tenacious girl, Mira Williams. I hope this little one has as much heart as you when she's your age."

My smile widened when she handed over two twenties.

"Sabrina and I can't wait for you to come help watch her tomorrow. Maybe I'll make a dinner that doesn't come from a box." Mrs. B laughed. "And I'd love to continue our conversation about Einstein's theories, like how black holes make orbiting matter wobble."

"Yeah, and gravitational waves!"

Ever since I'd started helping with Sabrina, our space talks had picked up again.

I thought about that day when I'd heard Mrs. B over the baby monitor and she'd called me a "mad scientist." The comment still stung, but I kind of understood now what she meant.

Helping out with Sabrina for a few hours a week was exhausting. I couldn't imagine spending twenty-four hours a day, every day with her. Mrs. B's words might have been blunt, but she hadn't said it like the way I always called Tamika an annoying evil scientist.

When Mrs. B had finally gotten a second of peace, the loud, obnoxious music had broken the silence. Waking up Sabrina. Once again Mrs. B had had to soothe the forever-wailing little one.

"Good luck with the fundraiser, Mira." Mrs. B waved as I skipped down her driveway.

House after house that first hour was full of praises for my courageous efforts and full of well wishes for Sir Fig Newton.

"Good for you, taking action." Five dollars.

"Oh, your poor kitty." Ten dollars.

"Wishing you and your family all the best." Twenty dollars.

Even Mr. Spencer, our quiet neighbor, donated a check for fifteen dollars. His hairy knuckles rubbed against his stubbled chin. "My brother-in-law has diabetes. Who knew cats could get it too?"

With each donation the warm tingle that had started in my chest at Tamika's house spread down my arms, until it tickled my entire body. I'd collected $175 from twelve houses! That was more money in one hour than after two days with the lemonade stand.

My standard response, "Sir Fig Newton and I thank you so much," never felt like enough. I wanted to hug everyone and do cartwheels and skip down the block singing, *Everything's really gonna be all good!*

But then the farther from home I got, the more doorbells started to go unanswered. I made a note to try those houses again the next day but left flyers tucked in mailboxes just to be safe.

I pulled my curls into a bun. My frizz had shrunk at least two inches, thanks to the humid air. My speech remained the same, but my excitement evaporated into discouragement. "My name's Mira Williams and my cat, Sir Fig Newton, was diagnosed with diabetes. I'll be biking six miles through our town to raise money for his treatment. Any amount you give will make a difference."

"Sorry but . . . I don't have one bill to spare." Sympathetic face.

"Sorry but . . . I just gave to this other kid for this other thing." Shoulder shrug.

"Sorry but . . . I'm allergic to cats." Door shut.

Mom and Dad were right. This was much harder than I'd imagined. Even though there were still a couple of weeks left, I'd already gone to most of the houses in my neighborhood. And I wasn't even halfway to $1,000. What if no one else would help?

I wiped the sweat from my brow. How could I tell Fig, *Sorry, we're sending you away to live with someone else?* My body shuddered. I'd had enough of all the big, stupid buts for one afternoon.

I headed straight home. Dad was busy making dinner, so I snatched the laptop from his recliner. Although I'd dodged Thomas's weekly phone call and still hadn't emailed him back, I didn't know where else to turn.

From: Mira Williams

To: Thomas Thompson

Date: Jul 12, 4:22 PM

Subject: RE: How's Camp?

Hey.

Happy to hear things are looking up in DC.

Things are not so great here.

I've been going door-to-door all day asking

for donations for my Operation Save Fig bike

ride in two weeks, but I don't think I'll ever raise
enough to keep Sir Fig Newton at home. I don't
know what else to do.

I really wish I could come visit, but my dad
still doesn't have a job yet. Maybe you can come
down to Florida and help? I bet together we
could save Fig.

Write soon,

Mira

After hitting send, I crashed on my bed and snuggled into Fig as he slept. My body tensed as I caught a whiff of his sweet-smelling breath.

If only I could play a head-bopping song that would put an end to this incurable disease. For people *and* cats. The facts might point to no cure, but if scientists let every obstacle get in their way, then there'd never be any major scientific discoveries. It's all about the science of persistence. I may have pressed pause on curing my parents' blues with my mood-music playlist, but I couldn't quit on Operation Save Fig.

"On a scale of one to ten," I said to Fig, "rate your current stress level."

Fig's eyes struggled open to meet my gaze. His look expressed deep disapproval.

"Well?"

Fig's white-tipped tail tapped against the bed three times.

"How would you describe your current mood?"

His face clearly read: *Purr-lease, it's nap time.*

I put my hand over his left side, just behind his front leg, and counted the number of heartbeats in fifteen seconds. Thirty-eight beats times four equaled 152 beats per minute. Fig's heart rate was normal, even on the low end, just like a relaxed cat's. But Fig wasn't like Mrs. Branson. She'd been aware of all that was wrong in her world when she was a subject in my Save Dad from His Funk project.

Frustrated and antsy, I snuck a peek at my email account. I was surprised to find a reply.

From: Thomas Thompson

To: Mira Williams

Date: Jul 12, 4:38 PM

Subject: RE: How's Camp?

I gave some of my allowance back to my
mom to write a check for Fig. It's not a lot, but
hopefully it'll help.

Sad to hear you can't visit. My mom said
we probably won't be coming back to Florida
anytime soon. Maybe when your dad gets a
new job, then you can come. Maybe during
Christmas break? Pete was telling me about the
Smithsonian's ZooLights Express and ice-skating
at the national Sculpture Garden. That would be
awesome if you could join us. I hope it'll snow.
Like a real white Christmas. You don't get those
in Florida.

Thomas

I snapped the laptop shut and checked my own pulse.
The slow rate indicated that the black hole's gravitational pull was growing stronger. I recalled from my
music research that enjoyable music stimulates the pro-
duction of the hormone serotonin, which makes us feel
joy and elevates our moods by altering our brain waves.
I hit play on my iPod, and Pharrell's "Happy" rattled the

speakers. I twirled around the room. But even with every shake and shimmy, my brain waves remained flatlined.

Sir Fig Newton's tail wobbled along off beat. Maybe if I just lost myself in the music . . . Maybe if I ignored the awful, horrible, heavy stuff hovering over me . . . Maybe, if I just believed . . . I imagined every note worming its way into his gray body, killing any and all traces of his diabetes.

My problems felt big, but music felt so much bigger. I'd already proven with Gran and Mrs. B that it could improve your mood. As I swayed, I imagined that music could actually heal. That it could be blasted over a packed auditorium, soulful sound waves sweeping over and drowning out all that was bad. Ending all diseases and the common cold with a single song.

There had to be a faster way to raise enough money in time. Mrs. Smith had said she always asked for more, to go big. I was moving at negative velocity going door-to-door. If only I could plead to a packed auditorium, then, just maybe . . .

My head-bopping stopped. Big bang, that was it!

25

MY TERRIBLE, AWFUL, ABSURD IDEA

Overhead fans whirled at maximum speed, cutting through the humid summer funk. Gran and I snagged her usual spot—third row, right-hand side, on the aisle—and parked on the wooden bench.

I'd spoken with Gran the weekend before, about my latest plan to save Sir Fig Newton, and she was totally on board. "Ask and it shall be given. My church is my community, and you're my family, so of course they'd love to hear from you."

I hoped Gran was right. Even though I'd raised some

more money over the past week with my babysitting gig and doing more door-to-door donation requests, I was still a long way off from my goal.

Gossiping folks, dressed to impress in snazzy gear and bedazzled hats, piled into the church. Miss Nora stopped by and greeted Gran. Before she left, she added with a wink, "Looking forward to your big announcement today, Mira." My body jerked as I remembered how awful my last public speech had gone.

Once the organ began to hum, the chatter muted and everyone took a seat. The congregation sang along with the choir for an eye-rolling half hour. I tried joining in, to forget about my terrible, awful, absurd idea, but when I sang, "Great Is Thy Faithfulness," my voice splintered in my throat and came out a garbled, high-pitched mess. I pressed my palms against my bouncing knees instead.

After the singing ended, Pastor Robinson strutted onto the stage. His deep, rhythmic voice thundered through the hall. "My Lord"—his arms were spread open wide before the congregation—"your Lord, works in mysterious ways."

Hands waved in the air, followed by random shouts of "Amen" and "Praise Jesus."

I perched on the edge of the wooden bench, my head propped in my hands. All I could think about was what I was going to say. There was one week left to raise over $500, and I couldn't . . . no, I *wouldn't* let Fig down. With my thoughts bouncing between my restless nerves and persistent determination, I missed the pastor's entire sermon.

"Before we leave today, I ask that you give your attention to a courageous girl. Many of you know our longtime member Ms. Elmira Williams and her lip-smacking greens. Her granddaughter would like a moment of your time. Please, give your attention to our young sister, Mira Williams."

My body froze. Ready to flee, I looked at Gran. Even though her church members were nice, especially Miss Nora, I didn't really know these people. What if they could tell I didn't believe in God? What if they hated me? Or worse, what if they were allergic to cats? This was a horrible idea.

Gran gave me a firm nod. "Make me proud."

I breathed in deep and forced my Jell-O legs onto the stage. Pastor Robinson handed me the mic, and I faced the crowd. Ready-to-go-home faces stared back at me.

"Hello." My wobbly voice squeaked, and the speaker

shot out feedback. Both the crowd and I winced.

I pulled the mic a little farther from my face. I took a slow breath and dug deep.

"I was here a month ago when the pastor talked about faith. I remember when he said that Jesus told Jairus, 'Don't be afraid; just believe.' The fact is, my cat, Sir Fig Newton, a member of my family for almost six years, is sick. He has diabetes. And just like for people, there's no cure."

Creaking benches, murmurs, and a few gasps rumbled through the church.

"But there *is* treatment," I said, my voice picking up bass. "Sir Fig Newton needs special food and insulin to get his blood sugar normal. But his treatment costs more money than my allowance. More money than my parents have. I'm trying to stay strong for Fig. I have faith that with his treatment, Fig will be his old self again."

I might not have believed that Jesus created zombies, but I did believe in fighting for Fig. I paused and looked at the pastor. He swiped his hankie across his slick forehead and waved me on with a bouncing nod and smile.

"So." I cleared my throat. "Next Sunday I'll be biking six miles through my hometown to raise money for his speedy recovery. And if any of you are interested in supporting me and Sir Fig Newton, then let me or my gran know. Just ten dollars, five dollars, even one dollar can make a difference. Thanks."

Pastor Robinson wrapped a bulky arm around my shoulder before I could run off.

"C'mon and show some love for this brave little girl and her cat," the pastor said, ushering me off the stage.

The church boomed with applause.

After the service a small mob, mainly moms with their kids, and of course Miss Nora, swarmed around Gran and me. My enthusiasm skyrocketed.

"Such a brave young girl."

"You must be so proud, Ms. Elmira, to have such a strong granddaughter."

"I'll pray for you and your poor kitty."

Some took flyers, promising to spread the word. I collected a few donations, but nowhere close to what I'd need to save the day, as I'd hoped. My lightness eclipsed. Although I appreciated their prayers, Fig needed their dollars. $591.74 to be exact.

Gran and I started toward her Oldsmobile.

"Mira, wait," an unfamiliar voice called.

"Thanks for all the prayers and stuff," I said on autopilot, turning to hold out a flyer.

My eyebrows flew up. Gran's nemesis was running up to us, her shiny black heels clicking against the pavement. Dressed in a red designer suit with matching lipstick, she appeared as if she'd walked right out of the TV studio, polished and camera-ready. Her palm ran over her straightened hair curled at her shoulders, smoothing down any flyaways.

"My name's Gervean Campbell and—"

"We *know* who you are." Gran's curt tone hacked through her introduction.

Ms. Campbell startled, but she quickly regained her composure. "Well, I was really moved by your plea, sweetie. You must've woken up the journalist in me. I recorded your speech." She waved her phone with a smile.

"In God's house?" Gran frowned.

Ms. Campbell ignored her. "I have a YouTube channel now called *Black, Vegan, and Proud.* You and Sir Fig Newton's fight against diabetes would be absolutely perfect for my vlog. I'd love to share your story in my next episode, maybe even interview you live, with your permission, of course."

My entire being did a triple-decker somersault. "That would be—"

"Something we'd have to ask her parents," Gran said, interrupting me. "But thank you very much for the opportunity, Ms. Campbell."

"Of course." She handed Gran her business card and shook my hand.

"Good luck to you, Mira. I hope to hear from you soon."

As soon as she walked away, Gran's face split into a huge grin and she hugged my shoulders. "A celebrity is going to share my grandbaby's story!" she bragged. Gran had never displayed this much excitement before, neither in tone nor on her face. Not even during Sunday service.

"But I thought we had to talk to Mom and Dad first?"

Gran waved her hand. "I'm sure they'll be fine with it. I just said that to keep Ms. Gucci on her toes. Anything to save Sir Fig Newton, right?"

"Right," I said.

"Tell me one thing, though." Gran's nose wrinkled as if she'd caught a whiff of Dad's cooking. "What's a vlog?"

26

MORE THAN SATISFACTORY

After Gran had shared the former news anchor's proposal, my parents scoped out Ms. Campbell's online video blog, *Black, Vegan, and Proud*, before giving the okay. I took a peek over their shoulders too. Ms. Campbell had done a piece on Channel 2 News about type 2 diabetes in the Black community and had wanted to spread the word after she retired on how what we eat and our physical activity could prevent the disease. So she'd started the YouTube channel.

The day before her episode on me and Fig, I sat at

my desk, the family laptop opened to her YouTube channel home page. There were tons of videos with titles
like "Vegan Soul Food *Does* Exist," "Black Beauty in
All Shades," and "Birth of an Animal Rights Activist." I
rubbed the back of my neck, staring at the number underneath the vlog's title: 275k. She might not have been a
mega influencer with millions of followers, but she had
almost THREE HUNDRED THOUSAND subscribers!

My eyes squeezed shut as I remembered when I'd
totally blanked during the group presentation at STEM
Girls camp. And then Tamika had stepped in. What if I
froze while Ms. Campbell interviewed me—*live*—on her
vlog? Tamika wouldn't be there to save the day. And this
was way more important than the app presentation. I
couldn't let Sir Fig Newton down.

When my eyes opened, I spotted the card Thomas had
sent, along with a ten-dollar check to help out with Fig.

On the cover was a black-and-white photograph of a
woman wearing an aviator hat and a long leather coat.
She stood on the wheel of one of those World War One
propeller planes, with a look of determination, as if fueled
by miranium. Underneath, bold letters read:

WOMEN WHO DEFY

Before Amelia Earhart flew solo across the Atlantic,
when American flight schools didn't admit African
Americans or women, thanks to her tenacity Bessie
Coleman became the first woman of African American
and Native American descent to earn a pilot's license.
Follow your dreams and soar the skies like Queen Bess.
Learn the stories of aviation and spaceflight at
The National Air and Space Museum

I opened the card, wondering if Thomas had been with
Pete when he'd bought it. Inside were the words "I know
you'll make your goal. You're Miranium!"

Biting the inside of my cheek, I wondered, *Will I raise
enough money in time?*

What if during my interview I forgot Fig's name or kept
saying "uh" and "um" and nothing else while my entire
face burned red? Or what if I ended up saying something
silly and became the "joke clip of the week"?

Maybe Thomas could help me practice so that I'd be
absolutely, without-a-doubt ready. I logged into my email
account. My shoulders slumped. Thomas wasn't online.
And today was supposed to be our weekly chat, and he

hadn't called. Just like last week. He was probably getting basketball lessons from Pete.

My gaze darted back to his card. I thought about Tamika, when Becky had introduced her at STEM Girls camp. She'd shared that Tamika wanted to be a pilot, just like her uncle. Grinning, I tried to picture her with an aviator hat and imagined her still wearing her ginormous flower poking out the side. Poppy's words, "It's nice when someone has your back," popped into my head.

That was when I noticed that everyone from Team Apptitude was online! I sent Poppy, Becky, and Tamika a link to join me on a video chat, along with the message *PLEASE HELP!* In less than a minute all four of our heads appeared on-screen, each in their own box, forming one gigantic square.

"Ohmygosh, hello, everybody!" Becky squealed, flipping back her long black hair, this time showing off dangling earrings.

"Hey, *El*mira. Flabbergasted to hear from you." Tamika wore her usual smug grin, while adjusting her gigantic white flower.

Poppy gave a small smile.

"You're probably wondering why I reached out," I said.

With a deep breath I caught everyone up on my dire situation. About Sir Fig Newton's diabetes diagnosis, having less than a week to raise enough money for his treatment, and my live interview with Ms. Campbell the next day.

"So, that's where you guys come in," I continued. "We were such an awesome team at camp, and, well, I can't mess this up. Would you guys help me practice for my interview?"

"Definitely!" Becky said.

"What a prodigious idea," Tamika said, this time wearing a real big grin, like the one she had in the picture with her uncle at the science center.

Poppy nodded enthusiastically.

"Great," I said. "Who wants to go first?"

For over an hour everyone took turns asking me questions, *even* Poppy.

"How did you know that Sir Fig Newton was sick? I mean, can cats really get diabetes?"

"Why do you need *so* much money?"

"Do cats really have nine lives?"

"Why a bike-a-thon?"

"How old's Fig? Is it like dogs, where one year for a dog is way more in human years?"

I stumbled a bit in the beginning, but even though my cheeks kept growing hot, I never froze once! The more questions they asked, the more comfortable I got. I did say "uh" and "um" a lot, but that was okay. Becky pointed out that it gave me a chance to pause and think about what I wanted to say.

We kept on chatting about fun stuff, like our favorite movies, books, and songs. Surprisingly, Tamika didn't talk about her science fair experiment. Instead she told us about the time her uncle took her flying in one of those "single-engine, four-seater planes."

"Did you get to wear an aviator hat?" I asked, glancing at the card from Thomas.

"No," Tamika said, her face scrunched up like she was confused but wanted to smile, "but that would've been stupendous."

Becky showed off her favorite matching necklace and earrings—"It's my birthstone, yellow topaz"—followed by some of the seashells she'd found at the beach. She held against her ear a brownish-orange-and-white-striped conch shell, slightly larger than her hand, and said, giggling, "Hey, Ariel, I can't hear you over the ocean waves."

"Ask her what's happening under the sea," I said, and we all died laughing.

Trying to catch my breath, I started to feel bad that I could have such a good time without Thomas. I wondered if this was how he felt whenever he hung out with Pete. Or did he not even think about me at all?

Suddenly Fig jumped up onto my desk and planted himself on top of the keyboard. The entire group burst into a harmony of "Awwwww."

"My mom's calling me for dinner," Becky said, "but don't worry about tomorrow, Mira. You've got this!"

Tamika nodded. "You did more than satisfactory today. Tomorrow you'll do great."

Poppy gave two thumbs-up.

"Thanks, guys." My cheeks flushed.

Poppy's shy smile widened. "That's what friends are for."

✦✧ 27 ✦✧

MY SUPERHERO

The following evening my parents and I crowded around the laptop at the dining room table. Dad nervously drummed his fingers on the tabletop. While bringing up the *Black, Vegan, and Proud* YouTube channel, I sat hunched forward, mere inches from the screen. Mom gently pulled me back with a warning that I was in that territory where I would surely mess up my eyesight. Sir Fig Newton nestled in my lap.

I wondered if he knew that something monumental was about to happen.

Earlier in the day Dad and I had spoken with Ms. Campbell about how the interview was going to work. Tonight's episode went live at five and usually lasted about an hour. After she showed the video of me speaking at Gran's church, then we would do the interview using Zoom.

"Remember," Ms. Campbell had said, "this is just a relaxed conversation, no more than five, ten minutes, between two strong Black girls. So have fun with it."

I'd nodded, the butterflies in my stomach swarming.

"Just be sure to mute the YouTube video before we chat, so we don't get feedback. Don't worry about a thing, Mira." Ms. Campbell had flashed her brilliant white smile. "You'll be great!"

Resting my hands on my belly now, I could feel the butterfly wings start to flutter again.

Mom handed Dad a cup of tea, me hot chocolate, and set out a plate of my favorite, Mom's chocolate chip oatmeal cookies. Snacks before dinner? This was definitely a special event.

With ten minutes before showtime, I clicked on the channel's most recent episode, titled: "My Superhero

Mira and Her Cat." The video display popped onto the screen with the words "*Black, Vegan, and Proud* starting soon" on a black background and a live chat box to the right. I tried reading the comments, but the fast-moving feed made my eyes dizzy.

"Look," Mom said, pointing. "There are over six thousand people online!"

I nibbled on a cookie, but promptly put it down. My tummy was too nervous to enjoy it.

Suddenly the button next to the word "LIVE" flashed red. Ms. Campbell's face appeared on the screen. "Hello, beautiful people. It's your girl, Gervean Campbell, and welcome to another edition of *Black, Vegan, and Proud*."

The title was spelled out in cursive over a photo montage of Ms. Campbell dining with famous Black vegans like Coretta Scott King and the Williams tennis sisters, with a funky jazz beat kicking in the background. Ms. Campbell returned, sitting in what appeared to be her living room. The all-white furniture, accented with black animal sculptures and black-and-white paintings, was as polished and camera-ready as she was in her cream pantsuit.

Ms. Campbell started off talking about the vegan recipe of the week and then moved on to responding to comments from last week's episode. My body bounced in my seat, my nerves stretching with each passing second.

"Sometimes life throws you a curveball," she said, her face and tone cheerful, "but rather than give up or get mad, there's one young girl in my town who's taking action. You all know about my love for animals and my continuing crusade to put an end to diabetes. I was fortunate enough to cross paths with this amazing young person at church, and I'm so excited to introduce you to my new hero, twelve-year-old Mira Williams."

"That's me!" I squealed. Mom whooped beside me.

The screen switched to a shaky video of my speech at Gran's church.

"The fact is, my cat, Sir Fig Newton, a member of my family for almost six years, is sick. He has diabetes. And just like for people, there's no cure."

"That's my girl!" Dad jumped up and broke into the Cabbage Patch dance, swinging his arms in a circular, counterclockwise motion. I rolled my eyes at him but couldn't stop grinning.

Once the video of my speech finished playing, I quickly muted the live YouTube video and switched to another window where the Zoom call was already loaded. Ms. Campbell once again gave her famous bright-white smile.

"Welcome, Mira! Thanks so much for taking time to chat with me this evening."

"Hi," my voice squeaked as I awkwardly waved. "Thanks for having me."

Sir Fig Newton woke from his slumber and sat up in my lap. His gray ears showed up in my video screen.

"Is that the famous Sir Fig Newton?" Ms. Campbell asked.

Nodding, I lifted Fig up so everyone could see his lime-green eyes and round cheeks.

Ms. Campbell laughed. "What a handsome boy!"

After a few seconds Fig promptly squirmed out of my grip and leapt onto the floor. He plopped down on top of my bare feet.

"So, Mira, during your plea at church last Sunday, you mentioned faith. Do you have faith that you'll raise enough money by this weekend for Sir Fig Newton's treatment?"

I could feel the heat creep up my face and across my chest. I snuck a glance at Dad, then Mom. They both delivered vigorous nods with hopeful smiles.

Breathing in deeply, I turned back to the screen. "No matter how much money I raise, I have faith that my family and friends will always have my back, and Fig's."

Mom squeezed my knee and Dad patted my shoulder.

"Beautiful," Ms. Campbell said.

As our conversation continued, my jittery nerves and the butterflies floated away. It started to feel like I was talking with an old friend. I completely forgot that there was a live audience, and I started having fun.

"Just one more question, Mira." Ms. Campbell leaned forward with a serious face. "How did you come up with such a fabulous name as 'Sir Fig Newton'?"

"Everybody knows that Einstein's the greatest scientist in the universe, and someday I hope to be the same."

I wiggled my big toe. Sir Fig grunted but stayed snoozing on my feet.

"And every great scientist needs an awesome assistant, so I started calling him 'Sir Isaac Newton,' but my dad kept saying 'Fig Newton,' even though he says he's never eaten one in his life, and well, the two names smooshed into one and it stuck!"

"That's hilarious, Mira. Thanks so much for sharing your story with everyone today. I know one day you'll make an amazing scientist, and I wish you all the best at your bike-a-thon this Sunday."

The Zoom call ended, and I switched back to the window with the live YouTube video streaming. The screen faded to a brilliant blue and my bike-a-thon flyer appeared. Ms. Campbell's overenthusiastic voice announced, "If you are as excited as I am to support Mira and her cause, then please click the link to donate. Just like Mira said, any amount you give will make a difference. I have faith that my viewers won't let her or Sir Fig Newton down.

"As always, please give a shout-out in the comments below. Until next time, be true, be bold, be you."

Mom and Dad exploded with cheers and applause, waking Fig from his peaceful slumber and sending him lumbering down the hall. I leapt to my feet and bowed for my audience.

"Great job, Mira girl," Dad said.

Mom swallowed me in a tight hug. "Honey, I'm so proud of you."

Cookies before dinner *and* gushing admiration? A girl could get used to this *super*star treatment.

28

PEDAL TO THE METAL

O ver the next three days the praise continued for my plea to save Sir Fig Newton. Gran called to congratulate my "noble efforts," then scoffed when I was shocked that she'd actually seen Ms. Campbell's vlog.

"I may be old, but I'm not dead yet, honey."

Turned out she'd watched the *Black, Vegan, and Proud* episode on Miss Nora's computer. She said she'd called to make sure that I "didn't get too big for your britches." I assured her that my jeans fit just fine.

244

"I have faith, Miss Mira, that you'll reach your goal, God willing."

Several members from Gran's church were so impressed that she collected around a hundred dollars. Mom shared the video at work, and her coworkers chipped in too. My neighbor Mrs. B raved about living next door to an online celebrity and said she'd talked me up at her Mommy and Me class and forwarded my flyer to her friends at NASA. Even my favorite teacher, Miss Kirker, saw the video and called to offer her support.

I also received three separate emails from my Apptitude team members. Becky congratulated me on my "excellent" interview. And Poppy sent a video she'd made of a cartoon cat dancing and then holding up a sign at the end saying, GOOD LUCK ON YOUR BIKE-A-THON! My eyes widened in surprise after reading Tamika's words.

Your interview was way more than satisfactory. You were stupendous.

The days zipped by and the moment finally arrived. Today was the Operation Save Fig bike-a-thon!

At last count my Einstein piggy bank held $660.26. Not bad work for a persistent twelve-year-old, but still not enough. If I didn't collect over $300 by tomorrow, then . . .

I refused to let the thought in.

I leaned over Fig, snoozing on my unmade bed, and kissed his snout. He didn't stir, but his Hershey breath fueled my energy. I got my bike from the garage and waved to my parents standing on the front porch as I coasted down the driveway.

Dad beamed. "Good luck."

"See you at the finish line," Mom said.

Even though it was eight in the morning, the sun was already melting the pavement. Just my luck. I'd picked the hottest, most humid day of summer. I repositioned my bike helmet, my curls tied in a low bun underneath, confident I was protected by my oversized sunglasses and a generous slathering of sunblock insisted on by Mom. I rolled my eyes. My natural tan never burned like her fair white skin.

I pedaled down the block toward the front entrance of my neighborhood. It was oddly quiet. No cars, no barking dogs, no rustling leaves. Not one peep. It was as if an asteroid seven miles wide had hit Earth, and only the greatest scientist in the entire universe had survived the destruction. Of course I knew this wasn't the case. Otherwise, there'd be fireballs raining down and smoke and dust blocking the sun, making the sky pitch-black. All humans—including me—would be wiped out, just like the dinosaurs.

I turned the corner, finally stumbling upon life. Mr. Spencer was out watering his lawn.

I exited the subdivision and turned right onto the main road, slim with Sunday morning traffic. I wiped the pooling sweat from my forehead. My first stop: Kennedy Middle School. Thomas and I had been so excited to start seventh grade together. This would be the year I'd win the science fair. And Thomas would shake off his "Brick" nickname and make the basketball team. The first day of school was only a month away.

But Thomas had moved on without me, and was getting b-ball lessons from his new friend, Pete. My grip tightened around the handlebars. Thomas hadn't called the past two weeks. I'd emailed him the link to Ms. Campbell's vlog with my video and received a three-word email response: *Cool!!! Good luck.*

Did Thomas even care anymore?

Maybe it was time to embrace the facts. Maybe my friendship with Thomas had expired.

My legs pumped faster, cranking up a breeze.

After about five minutes I arrived at my destination. My neighbor Mrs. B and Tamika's mother were standing together in the school parking lot. Mrs. Branson was waving her arms in the air, a snot-oozing Sabrina wriggling in a baby wrap against her chest. Mrs. Smith held a yellow poster high above her head.

"Woo-hoo!" Mrs. B said, forcing Sabrina's clenched hand into a fist pump. Sabrina offered her opinion with a toe-curling shriek. Then Mrs. B yelled, "You've got this!"

"Way to go, Mira," Mrs. Smith said. Her sign read: GO, OPERATION SAVE SIR FIG NEWTON! WE BELIEVE IN YOU!

A flicker of appreciation ignited across my chest, yet oddly the spark fizzled out. It was weird seeing Mrs. Smith without Tamika. So much for her having my back. I'd thought maybe, after her help with the vlog interview and her encouraging support, that she'd be here. But no. Of course Tamika wouldn't show up. She'd tried to poison me with not-spicy chicken soup, right?

I shook my head and guzzled down half a bottle of water.

Pedal to the metal, I took off again. My tiny entourage's cheers faded as I continued down the main road toward my next stop and one of my favorite hangouts, the public library.

I skidded to a stop in the parking lot. My jaw dropped. A crowd huddled in the shade of the front entrance, chanting "Go, Mira! Save Sir Fig."

A woman in a gold dress with a matching floppy sun hat and flip-flops looked familiar. She was a sunburst in the rift of strangers. I ditched my bike on the sidewalk and was approaching my fans when it finally clicked. It was the librarian from near Gran's house, Tickled Pink, who'd helped me find "The Silent Cat Killer" article! Though, I guess now I should call her Tickled Blonde.

I slipped off my sunglasses. "I-I can't believe you're here!"

"Of course I am." Her face brightened as she grinned. "When I saw your interview online, I remembered you and the printer fiasco."

"Yeah, sorry about that." I blushed sheepishly. "But . . . but that was all the way in Orlando!"

"Nonsense." Tickled Blonde waved her hand. "What's an hour drive when it comes to showing my support for such a worthy cause?"

The spark planted in my chest by Mrs. B and Mrs. Smith flared.

The rest of the fan club took turns expressing their admiration for my courageous fight, and their hope that Fig would beat this awful cat killer. I couldn't believe so many of them had seen the video!

"Such a big undertaking for such a young girl."

"Your parents must be so proud."

"You and Sir Fig Newton got this."

Away from the crowd, an older kid stood alone. His solemn face stared in my direction, his gaze vacant. He wasn't familiar at all, but his massive grief drew me to him, just like Newton's gravitational attraction. Once I stood in front of him, his eyes moved closer to me, but never made contact.

"Do I know you?" I asked.

"Saw your video," he mumbled, running a hand through his silky black hair. His eyes began to water, focused on his wringing hands. "I lost my dog, Biscuit, to cancer. We had to . . . for him, so . . . we let him go."

"I'm so sorry about Biscuit," I said softly, and not as one of those nice responses to make someone feel better. I really meant it.

He gave a slight shrug, his eyes still locked on his hands. "Just know you're not alone."

I retrieved my bike from the sidewalk, a wave of confusion drowning out the cheers from the crowd. My fingers pressed against my temples as a mass of thoughts played tug-of-war.

It's all good. The silent cat killer. You and Fig got this! There is no cure. Besties forever. Cool guy, Pete. We believe in you! The indisputable facts. We had to . . . let him go. If I don't raise enough money by tomorrow, they're going to give Fig away.

29

OH. MY. EINSTEIN.

Leaving the crowd in front of the library, I pedaled off in silence. My breathing labored as I struggled to push on with the Operation Save Fig bike-a-thon. I didn't want to be trapped in the void. Once you're caught in the gravitational pull, it's impossible to get out.

I rounded the corner. The next stop, Ashley's Restaurant, loomed ahead. Many locals and visitors believed the eerie tales of lights flickering on and off during the night, dishes falling on their own, and phantoms in the bathroom mirror. As the world's greatest scientist,

I wasn't afraid of ghosts. Why would they scare me? There was no scientific proof of their existence. Surely there was a rational explanation for all the incidents at Ashley's.

I encountered a repeat performance of unfamiliar fans cheering me on in front of the medieval, storybook-looking restaurant. Even some patrons, waitstaff, and cooks snuck out to see what the commotion was all about and then joined in the "Mira!" chant fest.

But the shouts did nothing to change my mood. Those haunting words snuck up on me again. *Cat killer. No cure. Had to . . . let him go.* Dread gripped my body. I shivered. Ghosts might not be real, but Fig being ripped from our home and given to another family scared me to death.

My eyes grazed over the crowd, not taking in any faces, until I spotted something familiar: an enormous white flower. Huh. I guess not everyone was a stranger.

Tamika broke from the crowd, pedaling forward until our bikes stood side by side. She held out an envelope.

I studied the front and back, not finding any markings. "What's this?"

"Just open it."

I tore it open and pulled out a single paper. Not just a paper, a *check*. A check for $100!

I stared at it with my mouth open. "But why?"

"I want you to reach your goal," Tamika said, and shrugged. "Us scientists need to stick together, like the hydrogen bonds of water, if we're going to put an end to, um, what'd you call it? The silent cat killer."

The flare in my chest reignited and spread like a rocket launch through my body, heating me from my scalp down to the tips of my toes. I just, I couldn't believe it!

Suddenly I thought of how awful I'd been to Tamika all summer. I shifted from side to side, staring at my sneakers. I'd accused her of trying to poison me to maintain her first-place status. And I'd doubted her intentions when she'd had my back during our app presentation. If she were so evil, would she have helped Fig and me out with such a large donation?

Hopeful, I looked her in the eye and asked, "Would you, maybe, want to join me?"

Tamika's shocked look quickly morphed into a smile. "Let's roll."

We headed out, waving to the crowd as we cruised

SIR FIG NEWTON AND THE SCIENCE OF PERSISTENCE

on to the final stop. We sped past the Publix shopping plaza, the wind whistling in my ears, and bounced over the train tracks.

Breaking the silence, Tamika said, "For knowledge is limited, whereas imagination embraces the entire world."

"Huh?"

She nodded down. "Your shirt."

Looking down, I saw the upside-down view of a cartoon Einstein staring back at me. It was my favorite shirt, the one from Thomas, with the famous "Imagination is more important than knowledge" quote printed on the back.

"That's not what it says," I said.

"No, but it's the rest of the quote."

My eyes bugged. The rest of the quote? I hadn't known there was more. How could Einstein's number one fan not know that?

Tamika continued in her singsong tone, "Another great quote was said by the greatest astronaut ever, Mae Jemison. 'Never be limited by other people's limited imaginations. . . . You've got to re-evaluate the world for yourself.'"

I nodded, letting her words sink in and fill me with purpose. My back lengthened. Just like miranium, I was indestructible.

Our steady roll began to slow as we climbed a hill. I crouched low, my breathing heavier, my heartbeat faster. The sun blazed. Sweat trickled down my neck, washing away my sunblock. Hmm, maybe I should conduct an experiment on whether or not sunscreen makes our sweat evaporate slower.

"C'mon, *El*mira," Tamika managed between heavy breaths. "We've got this."

With all the support I'd received from neighbors and strangers today, I was strangely upbeat. Even though I still hadn't raised enough money, my discouragement melted away. Gran was right about having faith in those who have your back. As we neared the top, I stood up from my seat, using all my weight to push down hard on the pedals.

The hill was tough, but not impossible, especially with Tamika huffing and puffing by my side.

Back on flat land, we entered the final stretch and gasped in unison. In front of the final destination,

Entenmann's Outlet Bakery, was the largest crowd all day. Friendly faces came into view, some familiar—Gran; my favorite teacher, Miss Kirker; the vet assistant with a tower of pumpkin-orange curls—along with gobs of strangers gathered in the parking lot.

Tamika and I parked in front of the crowd. I spotted Mrs. Lee, the teacher from STEM Girls, waving and wearing another fun shirt that read: SCIENCE IS MAGIC THAT'S REAL. Standing next to her was Ayana, the UCF grad student who'd talked about astronomy at camp. Turns out she was a huge fan of the *Black, Vegan, and Proud* vlog.

I slipped off my sunglasses as my gaze continued to roam over all the smiling faces. Suddenly I sucked in my breath. Becky and Poppy were holding a huge banner that read CONGRATULATIONS.

"Surprise!" They dropped the sign and tackled me with a group hug.

"I can't believe you guys came."

"Of course we did." Becky brushed aside her long hair, her diamond studs twinkling.

Poppy blushed. "Wouldn't miss it."

"So," Becky said, "what do you think of our awesome outfits?"

She and Poppy quickly posed, showcasing their bright red T-shirts.

A tingling started in my belly, kind of like butterfly wings, but the good-feeling kind. I read the words in large block letters out loud: "Team Apptitude."

My hand covered my gaping mouth as I finished silently reading the small cursive underneath, FINDING FUN & FRIENDS.

I felt a tapping on my shoulder and turned around. Tamika was holding out the same shirt. I took it, sniffing back happy tears.

"I can't believe you guys," I finally managed to say.

"It was T's idea," Becky said.

Before I had a chance to respond, Gran's nemesis, Gervean Campbell, came up holding a long selfie stick.

"Congratulations, Mira!" Ms. Campbell positioned herself next to me, her cell phone on the stick filming us both as she flashed a way-too-white smile. "How do you feel after completing your Operation Save Sir Fig Newton bike-a-thon?"

"I—I can't believe all the people who came out today," I said, holding the Team Apptitude shirt tight against my chest. "It's nice to know I'm not alone."

Ms. Campbell leaned in and nudged my shoulder. "Did you make your goal?"

There was a tug, but I kept my chin up. "No, but I still have faith."

"Well, maybe this will help." Ms. Campbell dipped into her bag and pulled out a check. My heart pounding, I took it. "This is from my viewers to you and Sir Fig Newton."

Oh. My. Einstein. The check was for $2,250! My knees buckled. I steadied myself against Tamika, whose eyebrows were up in her hair. With the $660 I'd raised before the bike-a-thon, plus the $100 from Tamika, and now this check from Ms. Campbell, I had more than enough money to keep Fig.

"Congratulations, Mira," Ms. Campbell said. "You are my hero."

"You did it!" Tamika said as we high-fived.

"We did it," I said, and smiled.

Ms. Campbell moved off to the side, still speaking into her phone with animated flair.

"Mira!" my dad called. He rushed over, a woman trailing behind in a red cape and tight shiny blue pants.

"There's my amazing girl," Dad said, thumping the top of my helmet.

"Ohmygosh," Becky squealed. "Is that . . . Wonder Woman?"

My eyebrows shot up once it registered who he was with. "Mom?"

She scooped me up into a tight hug. "I'm so proud of you, Mira."

She snuggled her face into my neck. Usually I'd be mortified at such over-the-top PDA, especially with her decked out in red boots, silver arm cuffs, and a gold belt, but today I didn't mind. Well, not as much as usual.

After an eternity or so, she let me go and held out plastic fangs, the same ones I'd given to her at the beginning of summer. "You get through the stuff you don't like with the ones you love."

A grin crept across my face as I took back the fake teeth.

"C'mon, let's eat," she said.

I peeled off my helmet and linked my arm through hers.

As the crowd surrounded us in the bakery parking lot,

everyone munching on free day-old doughnuts, I relished my relaxed state. The growing spark that had spread through my body had melted away my anxiety and doubt. Sir Fig Newton was still sick, but now that there was enough money, my parents, the vet, and I would do everything we could to make him better. And even more important, he would stay at home, where he belonged.

"You know what, Dad?" I said as I licked the sugary, white powder from my fingertips. "It's all good."

For the first time all summer, I believed it.

30

SMOOTH, QUICK, AND CONFIDENT

Fact: Every great scientist knows that an unproven theory isn't exactly science, but the idea that Sir Fig Newton would live a long, healthy life with the silent cat killer was about to come true. Scattered thunderstorms pummeled Florida's east coast, with wind gusts up to fifty miles per hour. The cloudy skies and pouring rain, however, couldn't dampen my sunny mood. Operation Save Sir Fig Newton had been a success, and today Fig would receive his first insulin shot.

The orange-curled vet assistant sailed into the Brevard

Animal Clinic's waiting room. "Sir Fig Newton?" she called.

I jumped to my feet, my wet umbrella in hand, and trailed behind Dad lugging Fig's carrier. A pathetic "mrow" drifted out. The vet lady ushered us into an exam room.

"Butter my cheeks and call me a biscuit, you were incredible last weekend," she said, and sighed in awe. "Sir Fig Newton sure is lucky to have you."

My heart lit up like a Bunsen burner.

Dad lowered the carrier onto the concrete floor next to the silver table looming in the center of the room. The vet assistant crouched low, peering into the carrier. Her head tilted from side to side, her mile-high bouffant swinging along.

"Welcome back, big fella," she cooed.

Fig cowered, motionless in the back corner.

She smiled sympathetically and dragged poor Fig out of his safety zone. After checking his heart rate, temperature, and weight, she announced, "Dr. Spires will be with y'all shortly." She swept out of the room as Fig dashed back into his carrier.

Within minutes Dr. Spires burst in with a booming, "Welcome, welcome."

"So"—his eyes grazed over the file in his hand—"today's the big day! We'll start Sir Fig Newton on insulin and get his blood sugar back in check."

"Yes, sirree. Thanks to my amazing girl here." Dad ruffled my curls.

Dr. Spires nodded. "I heard about your bike-a-thon, Mira. Congratulations."

I grinned sheepishly, leaning into Dad's wiry frame.

"Nice to have some good news for once," Dad said, his smile not quite outshining his overcast eyes. "Don't think I can handle any more financial cat-tastrophes."

The vet dragged Sir Fig Newton out of his carrier and plopped him onto the cold exam table. Fig's paws slid along the metal tabletop as he attempted an escape, but Dr. Spires managed to keep him in place. He poked and prodded Fig's trembling body, pausing every so often to scribble down notes.

The door opened and the vet assistant ducked inside. On the table near Fig she set down two small glass containers—one with a label, one without—two red-capped syringes, and an orange, and then she swiftly left the room.

An orange? Maybe Tamika and Mrs. Smith were right. Maybe OJ was a magic elixir.

All while keeping a wiggly Fig on the table, Dr. Spires picked up one syringe, removed the red cap, and turned his attention toward my dad. "Ready for your lesson?"

Dad's body froze, his wide eyes zeroing in on the thin, sharp point. I grabbed his hand, willing him to stay upright.

Dr. Spires's brows rose as he saw the color draining from Dad's face. My dad was like a thirteen-thousand-pound elephant freaking out over an itty-bitty African pygmy mouse.

"He's ready," I said firmly.

"Okay," Dr. Spires said, not sounding convinced. "Mira, please hold Sir Fig Newton still for me."

I reluctantly released Dad's clammy grip and clamped both hands on to Fig. His furry body struggled. Guilt pumped through my veins as his perturbed face read, *Traitor.* I tried to look sorry, but I couldn't manage it. This needed to happen.

"First," Dr. Spires said, "we fill the syringe with insulin." The vet gently rolled the labeled glass vial between the palms of his hands. "Don't shake it, you don't want air bubbles."

He held the vial upside down and inserted the needle through the rubber stopper.

"Be sure to draw the proper dose. We'll start him off on one unit, once a day, either while he's eating or after he's finished." As he pulled back on the plunger, insulin filled the syringe. He removed the needle from the vial. "Now you're ready to give the injection."

Dr. Spires held the syringe in his right hand and stroked Fig with his left. "Most important thing is to relax."

Dad nodded in slow motion, his terrified eyes locked on to the needle.

With his thumb and index finger, Dr. Spires grasped a fold of Fig's skin high on the back of the neck and pinched firmly, tenting the skin. "When you're ready to inject, try to be as quick, smooth, and confident as possible. You'll be an expert in no time."

The vet plunged the needle through the skin. Surprisingly, Fig had no reaction, not even a twitch, jerk, or howl. Dr. Spires pushed the plunger with his thumb and withdrew the needle. "It only takes a second," he said, replacing the orange cap. "Once the needle is through, he doesn't really feel a thing."

Dr. Spires gathered the unmarked vial, the unused syringe, and the orange and held them out to Dad. "Your turn."

Taking a slow, deep breath, Dad took the vial and rolled it slowly between his hands. His eyes closed for more than a few seconds. I imagined Dad silently chanting "It's all good" so he wouldn't faint. Or maybe hoping Fig would make a sudden recovery.

When his eyes opened, Dad grabbed the needle and filled the syringe with the proper dose. Holding the orange so tight, I swore juice would squirt out, Dad plunged the syringe forward. The needle struck the dimpled peel and bent sideways. Dad's face crumbled.

"And that's why we practice with water on an orange." Dr. Spires chuckled. He went to the towering cabinet against the far wall and pulled out a box. He passed the open container, filled with a bazillion syringes, to Dad. The room fell silent except for the wind howling outside.

Dad's body wavered. His gaze stuck on his kryptonite.

"Dad," I murmured. "Dad?"

His stance grew wobblier with each passing second, but somehow he managed to make eye contact with me.

"Dig down deep, Dad. Find that extra oomph."

His posture stiffened as my words appeared to sink in. He snatched a syringe, filled it, and plunged it—smooth, quick, and confident—into the orange.

"Excellent." Dr. Spires gave Dad two thumbs-ups.

Dad's face relaxed in relief. He looked sweaty, but he smiled. "Just a bit of oomph needed to get through an impossible situation."

Four days had passed since we'd started Sir Fig Newton on insulin and prescription food, and I was no longer annoyed by the 5:40-something a.m. meow alarm. We'd run through the same routine each morning, Fig's head hanging over my face, his unblinking stare screaming, *Feed me.* This morning was no different. Fig's pupils were so big that only a thin outer ring of lime green remained.

"Mrow. Mrow. Mrow."

His head slammed against my cheek with each catty remark.

I locked Fig into a snuggle and kissed his wet nose. I grinned. His sweet breath was gone.

"We did it, Fig," I whispered, holding his gray squirmy body. "You're getting better."

"Mmmmmm." Fig whined and shimmied until he wrestled from my grip. He tore off out of the room, no doubt to the kitchen.

I woke up Dad to give Fig his shot. Now a pro, Dad handled the needle with no hesitation. As he left for the family room, I stayed in the kitchen and watched Sir Fig Newton finish inhaling his prescription kibble. Although the vet had said it could take up to ten weekly visits to get his blood sugar in check, I was optimistic. He was hungry again.

My own stomach growling, I grabbed a packet of instant oatmeal. The sweet molasses smell of brown sugar teased my tongue as I placed the bowl in the microwave. My tummy's gurgles and grunts harmonized with the buzz. *Ten . . . nine . . . eight . . .* I remembered my Short-Circuit Scientist moment with Thomas and the exploding grapes.

Almost a month had passed since Thomas had last called—the call I'd avoided by pretending to be sick. His last email had only contained three words: "Cool!!! Good luck." No salutation. No sign-off. Not even a crummy joke.

Signaling the end, the microwave timer beeped three times. I snatched the warm bowl and settled at the dining room table. I shoveled a spoonful of oatmeal into my mouth and thought things over. Just because Thomas hadn't called in a while didn't mean we were no longer friends. Right? It wasn't like I'd been emailing him every day, and when I had emailed, it had always been about how things were going wrong. I hadn't exactly been the bestest friend either.

Everything I wanted to share with Thomas rushed through my mind: all the people at the bike-a-thon, raising enough money to save Sir Fig Newton, Fig's Hershey breath gone. These successes were meant to be shared with my best friend. I even wanted to say how sorry I was that I'd lied about being sick and refused his call.

My mind continued to spin as Sir Fig Newton plopped onto the dining table next to my empty breakfast bowl.

Fig's green eyes bore into mine. He head-butted my cheek. It was the push I needed.

Maybe if Thomas heard my voice, then he'd remember our promise of "best friends forever." Maybe our friendship could survive the light-years between us. All I needed to do was call him.

I snuck into the kitchen. Thankfully, Dad was still tucked away in the family room, focused on the laptop. After setting a ten-minute timer on the microwave, I lifted the phone from its cradle and dialed Thomas's number. My parents would kill me if they knew I was calling long distance, but hopefully they wouldn't notice if I kept the call under fifteen minutes.

I spun the spiral phone cord around my finger, tighter and tighter with each ring. My peanut-butter-colored skin turned a disturbing purplish pink.

"Hello?" a familiar voice answered.

"Thomas!" I gushed. The phone cord unwound from my finger, leaving crisscross indentations.

There was a second of silence. "Mira?"

"Oh my Einstein, I've missed you so much." My mouth accelerated into hyperdrive. "So much has happened.

My campaign going viral, Tamika showing up in my life way too many times to count, and you'll never believe it, but I raised enough money to save Fig!"

"That's great, but . . . this isn't a good time," Thomas said, sounding distracted. "Pete's here."

Pete. Of course. "Oh. Okay," I said softly.

"I'm glad everything's going to be okay with Sir Fig Newton. Did you get my check?"

"Yeah." My voice jumped up a pitch.

"Cool," Thomas said. "Got to go, but I'll call you back and you can tell me all about it."

"Yeah, sure. Call me back—"

The line went dead.

"Soon," I finished.

31

LOOK WHAT THE CAT PUKED UP

I stopped the timer on the microwave, the digits frozen on 9:01. The exact number of miles between Thomas and me. He'd picked Pete, not me. He'd even called me "Mira," instead of "Miranium." The more I kept thinking about it, the hotter and angrier I got. The pressure building inside was sure to explode.

I stomped to my bedroom and yanked the Kennedy Space Center photo from my dresser. Thomas and me, with Fig snuggled in my arms, along with two blobs where my parents used to be. Once again I ground the black

273

marker across the matte finish, this time until Thomas disappeared. My fury still raging, I grabbed a pair of scissors and snipped away until all the black holes were gone and I was alone.

I placed the shrunken photo back in the frame and sat cross-legged on my bed. Anger pounded and squeezed and bruised my heart. I'd never felt so lonely.

With a mumbling cry Sir Fig Newton bumped his head repeatedly against my leg. When I didn't respond, Fig nestled himself into my lap and looked up at me with his big eyes. My arms hung limp at my sides.

Fig released a high-pitched whimper.

I compelled my hand to stroke his fur, and Fig started his revved-up-engine purr. Slowly the mechanical petting softened and the shattered pieces in my heart began to fill. I leaned down and kissed the top of his head.

"You're right, Fig," I said. One by one, Team Apptitude popped into my thoughts. Poppy, Becky, and Tamika. "I'm not alone."

His tail shot straight into the air, swaying from side to side like a cobra.

Mrs. B had said that even though figuring out babies

was a LOT harder than making new and better space vehicles, she'd eventually figured out what every cry meant: *Feed my belly*; *Gas attack—burp me stat*; *Sleepy time*; *Stank alert—diaper change quick.*

Sir Fig Newton and I were no different. He always knew how I felt, and I'd gotten pretty good at figuring out most of his looks and quirks. Mrs. B had said that just because someone can't speak the same language doesn't mean we can't understand them. We just had to be patient and listen with our gut instead of our ears.

My gut might have been able to understand Sir Fig Newton, but it had no clue if Thomas and I would ever be friends again.

The following morning I woke up to Fig's head hanging over my face at the usual early hour. I interrupted his unblinking stare with a finger-to-nose boop. He sniffed my finger, then followed with a gentle love nip.

"Time to wake up Dad for your shot."

Fig leapt to the floor and paced at the closed bedroom door. I threw aside my blanket and planted my feet onto the—

"Ew."

Wet, sticky, mushy grossness.

I hopped on my dry foot all the way to the door and flipped on the lights. Great. A nice big pile of kitty vomit. I picked up a dirty sock and wiped my puke-covered foot clean.

I inspected the evidence. No hairballs. No plastic. Just Fig's expensive special-diet food.

Not good.

Sir Fig Newton gave me another nip, this time not so nice on my leg. I leaned down and checked him. He didn't seem thirsty, wasn't napping, didn't have the sugar breath. Other than trying to find the right insulin dosage to bring his blood sugar down, which could take almost three months, everything else was looking up for Fig. Why be worried over one little vomit?

Even though I wasn't at full rage, Fig must've felt my pain when my so-called best friend had hung up on me yesterday for his new best friend. My hypothesis: Fig had nervous-tummy syndrome.

I scooped up the cat puke and tossed the bunched-up paper towel into the garbage. I hugged my midsection, my indestructible miranium demeanor wavering. Nerves, that's what caused Fig to puke. It had to be.

After Fig's breakfast routine, I set a laser focus on the family laptop. With an hour left before my privileges were up and Dad would take back the computer, I was determined to finish compiling a feel-good playlist. Now that I'd saved Fig, it was time to do the same for Dad. I shuffled through a stack of his CDs, some from Gran's garage and a few I'd snuck from his collection at home. Every time I found the perfect song, I copied it from the disc onto the laptop.

With barely a minute to spare, the list was finally complete. I put a blank disc into the laptop and hit the button to burn the Save Dad from His Funk playlist. When it finished whirring, the tray popped open and I slipped the disc into a paper sleeve. Now it was time to test my other hypothesis. With the right music Dad could escape his zombified abyss.

I headed to the family room, the laptop and disc in hand. As expected, Dad was kicked back in his recliner, scrolling through his phone. Sir Fig Newton was curled on the floor by Dad's chair, soft wheezing snores accompanying his rising and falling tummy.

"Dad," I said, setting the laptop on the end table and holding the CD behind my back, "you know how things have been different ever since you lost your job?"

Dad's forehead wrinkled as he lowered his phone. Fig lazily raised his head, aiming his barely opened eyes in my direction. He gave a roaring-lion-wide yawn and then returned to his nap.

"You know, like, how you've been unhappy, staring at the job ads?" I waved at the laptop.

His head bobbed slowly, an eyebrow raised in confusion.

"Well, I made you something to help cheer you up."

I held out the CD. Dad rose from the recliner, decked out in his usual stuck-at-home uniform, a faded Fishbone concert tee and running shorts with worn-out elastic. He took the disc, and his brown eyes moved over the title scribbled on the cover in thick black ink: SAVE DAD FROM HIS FUNK.

A smile burst across his face. Almost as big as the one I'd erased from the Kennedy Space Center photo. He slipped the disc into the stereo and pushed play. His favorite song, "Give Up the Funk," blared. Fig startled.

Dad laughed and broke into the Running Man. I joined in, jumping, spinning, and sliding across the carpet. Even Fig shared our enthusiasm, his tail thumping along with the funky beat.

Dad and I cycled through all our favorite moves as if it were a dance-off. Dad's Electric Slide versus my Single Ladies. His moonwalk against my flossing. His Gangnam Style faced my Shoot moves. We closed out with Kid 'n Play's Kick Step until our ankles tangled and we dropped onto the carpet in hysterics.

"Thanks, Mira girl," Dad panted, ruffling my curls.

I grinned sheepishly and thought about our first visit to the vet and the huge bill he'd paid with the credit card, even though my parents didn't have the money. I hadn't saved Fig all on my own.

"Thank you, Dad."

"For what?"

"You know, for everything with Fig."

He swallowed me into a bear hug, then settled back in his chair, humming along with the CD still playing in the background, and picked up the laptop to resume his scrolling. I sashayed back toward my room, but stopped before the hallway to give Dad one final look. He was still smiling.

Life might not have been exactly the way it was that day at the Kennedy Space Center—Thomas was still in DC, hanging with his new friend, Pete; Mom still hated crunching numbers; and Dad was still out of work—but at least Dad was feeling better while on the job hunt. Even Mom was smiling more since she'd worn her Wonder Woman costume at my bike-a-thon.

I picked up the shrunken photo of Fig and me in front of the shuttle *Atlantis*. Despite the flash puke incident, Sir Fig Newton was getting better. My scientific efforts had caused awesome-sauce results. Mrs. Smith was right. You had to go big.

Suddenly I felt a nudge against my leg. Fig gazed up at me. *You know what you have to do.* I scratched under his chin, and his body stretched into my touch.

"You're right, Fig," I said. "There's someone else I have to thank."

32

JUST A SPOONFUL OF SUGAR

I slipped on my sneakers and Orlando Magic cap and headed down the block. A steady breeze offset the afternoon heat. The entire neighborhood was outside. Lawn mowers roared. Basketballs thudded against the pavement. Even the rustling leaves and swinging chimes voiced their joy for such a beautiful summer day.

Chaos was the science of surprise. And just like the clashing sounds were strangely relaxing, I never would've predicted my going back to this house. Especially with Thomas *really* gone. But it was the home of

the one person who'd been the biggest variable in helping me raise funds for Fig's treatment.

I knocked on Tamika's front door.

"*El*mira?" Tamika's brows rose.

"Hey, Tamika. Just came over to say . . ." I tugged on
my cap and forced a cough. "Thank you."

Her eyes widened. "For what?"

"For your mom's online fundraiser," I said. "If it wasn't
for her, and well, you and your big-dollar donation . . .
Everything with Sir Fig Newton is getting better."

"Glad to hear he's going to be okay." Tamika grinned.

I nodded, shoving away the sneaking reminder of this
morning's puking incident.

Tamika pulled the door fully open, eyeing me carefully like I might explode if she moved too fast. "Want
to come in?"

"Um . . ." My lips twisted out of shape, into some kind
of surprised-terror combination. My instinct was to blurt
out an emphatic NO, but the bike-a-thon had proved that
there was more to my rival than meets the eye without a
microscope. She waited patiently with a hopeful face.

I shrugged and followed Tamika up the inside stairs,

then bit back a twinge of sorrow as she bounded through a very familiar doorway. Of course she would've taken Thomas's old room, but it was weird being there without him. And even stranger being there with Tamika.

Was I betraying our friendship? I picked at my nails, my gut bubbling with guilt. So many fun times hanging out with Thomas danced through my mind— cannonballing into his pool, playing video games, and watching *Doctor Who.* I thought about that day at the Kennedy Space Center, and then how I'd removed Thomas from the picture.

My guilt bubble burst. Why should I feel bad? Thomas had erased me from his life first, replacing me with Pete. Right?

I stopped in the doorway, fascinated by the view before me. An inflatable solar system hung from the ceiling, with the sun and eight planets scaled to size, along with various starship *Enterprise* models. Posters of different shuttle launches, including *Columbia, Challenger,* and *Atlantis,* mixed in with various *Star Trek* posters of Nyota Uhura. There was even a life-sized cardboard figure of T'Challa's scientist sister, Shuri, from *Black Panther.*

Thomas's old room had thrown up in sci-fi.

I nodded in approval. "Very cool."

It really was *way* better than Thomas's LEGO model of the US Capitol building and framed Declaration of Independence print.

Tamika beamed. "My uncle built the starship models when he was a kid."

She cleared a space off her cluttered bed, and something clinked onto the floor.

"What's that?" I asked.

Tamika held up what looked like the supersized version of Fig's skinny insulin syringes. "If you think my hair's voluminous, you've never witnessed my cheeks after I ingest some nuts." She held the needle like a knife and swung the pen-like injector, then stopped just outside her thigh. "In case I eat any nuts by mistake, this EpiPen makes sure I don't die."

I wrapped my hands around my throat. "Like, *dead* die?"

She nodded. "But even more dire? Dairy makes me puke, and Doritos . . . let's just say it's quite atrocious."

"You're allergic to *Doritos*?" I frowned. "Tragic."

"Well, not technically allergic, but they give me

digestive issues that, um . . . You know like when tiny amounts of hydrogen, carbon dioxide, and methane combine with hydrogen sulfide and ammonia in the large intestine?" Tamika leaned in, her nose wrinkled. Her voice dropped to barely audible. "Let's just say I could put gas stations out of business."

I laughed so hard, I snorted. Tamika started to look offended, but then joined in.

"It's . . . no . . . laughing . . . matter," she managed between giggles.

With a few deep breaths, I got my hysterics under control.

"No pizza, no gooey brownies with nuts, and no Cool Ranch," I said. "Definitely not funny. How do you deal?"

"I just do." She shrugged. Her face turned mad serious. "How are you? Now that Thomas has moved?"

My jaw clenched. Why did she have to bring him up? Just when I was starting to forget. I opened my mouth to respond, but assorted emotions—anger, loneliness, jealousy, heartache—kept changing what I wanted to say.

After a long pause Tamika fiddled with the flower tucked behind her ear. "I really do appreciate you coming over."

"Us scientists must stick together." I gave a teeny smile, relieved by the topic change.

"Maybe, if you want, we could visit the *Journey to Space* exhibit at the science center before school starts. Or, maybe, ride our bikes again sometime?" she asked.

I tried to think of an excuse, but I didn't have one. I was even getting used to her silly white flower.

I slipped off my Magic hat and sat on her bed. "Sure, why not?"

A tap . . . rap . . . tap lazily pulled me out of sleep. I inhaled deeply—catching a whiff of cinnamon and bacon—and released a jaw-stretching yawn. My fists rubbed the crusted gunk from my eyes as the drumming against my window picked up to a steady beat. A low thunder burst rumbled, and my insides did the same.

I squinted into the dark and zeroed in on the glowing digits of my alarm clock. 7:00 a.m.! My leg jerked and knocked against Fig snoozing at the foot of my bed. He acknowledged with an irritated grumble.

Never in the history of Sir Fig Newton had he ever—and I mean never, ever—slept past his usual 5:40-ish head bump breakfast alarm. I wasn't surprised I'd slept in. Dad had jumbled my internal clock, thanks to our late-night marathon of *Doctor Who*—my favorite episodes with the brilliant and brave Martha Jones.

I knelt at the edge of my bed, hovering over Fig's gray mass of fur, afraid of what I might find. Yesterday had been his third weekly blood-sugar check. After his morning insulin shot and special-diet breakfast, Dad and I had dropped him off at the vet, where they'd measured his blood levels every few hours until Mom had picked him up on her way home from work.

Fig's blood sugar was still too high, so Dr. Spires had increased his daily insulin amount. But the vet had assured Mom that Fig appeared to be doing well, and like he'd said in the beginning, it could take some time before they found the right amount to get Fig's blood sugar normal. Everything should have been all good, right?

But Fig had thrown up twice now, the day after Thomas had hung up on me for Pete, and then again a week later, right after inhaling his dinner. Now he wasn't demanding his before-dawn breakfast. And despite the rolling thunder, he couldn't be bothered to hide under the covers. Something more serious than nervous-tummy syndrome was messing with Fig.

My bare feet dragged along the carpeted hall. Dad sat at the dining room table, staring at his phone, and there was a stack of French toast and a pile of bacon awaiting my arrival. My stomach gurgled excited approval, but my brain reminded my taste buds that this had been made by Dad's hands.

"Morning, sleepyhead," Dad said, spooning sugar into his coffee mug. "I was giving you five more minutes."

"What's all this for?" I waved my hand over the spread before assembling a small pile on my plate. Usually breakfast was a bowl filled with cold or hot cereal.

Dad shrugged. "Oh, I don't know. Maybe it's because my number-one-daughter-made playlist finally paid off." He winked. That's when I noticed the spark in his eyes. He wasn't wearing his usual stuck-at-home uniform. There was no more overgrown stubble and no dry, tangled 'fro. Instead he was freshly showered, clean-shaven,

Afro-picked, and wearing a short-sleeved button-down and khakis.

I grabbed his hairy knuckles and lifted up his arm. No more ashy elbows.

"Paid off?"

He nodded. "I have an interview tomorrow."

I gaped. "Awesome, Dad!"

"Looks like your playlist's my lucky charm."

Dad's contagious grin bloomed in my cheeks. This outcome proved my hypothesis. The right mix of music could save Dad from his funk.

Music, however, couldn't cure Sir Fig Newton. Whatever was going on with him.

"Who's ready for their insulin?" Dad looked down at the ground, then peered down the hall. "Where's Fig Newton?"

I smothered my breakfast in syrup, not sure if I should say anything. No telling how he'd react to spending more money for more tests. Dad might have had an interview, but he didn't have a new job yet.

Dad kept staring at me, waiting for a response. I managed to squeak, "Still sleeping."

Dad nodded. "Finish eating, and then we'll give him his shot. We still have time in the two-hour window."

I nibbled on the mushy, slightly charred bread. The never-ending rain pounded against the patio door, matching my rapid heartbeat. Maybe I could sugarcoat my fears in a way to make it easier for Dad to digest.

"You, um, you know how Dr. Spires said it could take a while before Fig's blood sugar is normal?"

"Uh-huh." Dad tore into his bacon. I hated to see that goofy grin go away, but it had to be done.

I stabbed a chunk of French toast with my fork and dragged it through the gooey syrup. "I think he's right, but it just seems to be taking way too long, like glacial speed."

"What do you mean?"

"I don't know." I paused and looked toward my bedroom, hoping Fig would come sprinting down the hall, meowing for his food, and quash my churning worries. "Like, maybe he's not really getting better after all."

He waved me off with a piece of bacon. "It's normal to be worried, Mira, especially when you want something fixed right away. You just have to be patient."

Lightning struck, casting a twenty-microsecond light show across the wall. Just like the air around a strike was about five times hotter than the surface of the sun, my face was superheated. It was one thing for Fig to get better at a sloth's stroll. It was another for him to grow worse overnight.

"Patience and hope, kiddo," Dad said. "The world's best medicine."

I forced a flat smile but really wanted to say, *What do you do when you finally get your hope back, then lose it all over again?*

33

A LEOPARD CAN CHANGE ITS SPOTS

Fact: Finding friends was *so* much more than finding fun. The following morning, Fig slept past his early-morning wake-up call again. So when Tamika invited me to go swimming at her house that afternoon, I figured a swim, and a friend, might help me feel better.

The sun had sucked away all the dampness and puddles from yesterday's thunderstorm. Floating on a yellow raft in Thomas's old pool, Tamika looked weird without her white flower behind her ear, her hair hidden under a snug bathing cap. Though, her signature petals were still represented by the oversized white daises covering her neon pink bathing suit.

Standing at the pool's edge, I jumped as high as I could and then quickly hugged my knees tight against my chest. I hit the water with a big *kerTHUNK*.

I rose to the surface, shaking out my curls. Tamika threw me a bewildered stare. "How peculiar. Never met a Black girl who gets her hair wet on purpose."

"Maybe I take after my mom." I shrugged. "Ever try putting talcum powder on yours?"

She screwed up her eyes real tight, like she was thinking hard about it. Once her brain calculated my reasoning, she grinned. "Funny. It's hydrophobic. The electric charges in the molecules won't let water stick."

"Too bad it doesn't actually work. But it does get rid of sweaty skin!" I smiled for the first time all day. It was kind of cool talking about science stuff with someone who was actually interested and understood.

"Can I ask a personal question?" Tamika asked.

"Uh, sure."

"Did you and Thomas . . . did you two ever kiss or anything?"

I laughed in shock. "Gross!" I wiped the back of my hand across my lips. "Thomas and I were best friends. He was like a brother."

"Sorry."

"Now, Jonathan Isaac from the Orlando Magic," I said with a heavy sigh, "I would definitely kiss him."

"I think Thomas is cute." Tamika grinned.

"Eww, gross."

"He is." Tamika shrugged. "You said, '*was* like a brother.' Are you two still friends?"

"No—yes—I don't know."

After an awkward pause Tamika broke the silence. "Um, so remember how I told you that I'd be exploring Kepler's third law for next year's science fair?" She rambled on about how a planet's distance from the sun was directly related to the speed at which it traveled. The farther away a planet, the greater its orbital period.

As Tamika babbled on, I thought about how much everything had changed. How Thomas was probably hanging with Pete. And how much fun I was having with Tamika.

I wasn't really angry anymore, but it still hurt when

I was reminded of him. It was *sort of* like Kepler's third law. The more Thomas and I were apart from each other, the longer it took for me to remember how much I missed him.

"It takes almost a hundred and sixty-five years for Neptune to complete one orbit around the sun!" Tamika gushed with excitement.

I shuddered. That was a long time. Would the distance between Thomas and me grow so large that I'd forget him completely?

Bending my knees at the shallow end, I arched my back until my head and shoulder blades were resting on the water. My legs and torso followed suit, and I pushed my foot against the pool's edge, which sent me floating in no fixed direction. If only moving through life could be this easy.

"You know how there was a time when we thought we would never travel faster than sound?" I asked. My head dipped under water, and my ears clogged.

"Yeah?" Tamika's reply was muffled. I swallowed hard, popping my ears.

"Do you think we'll ever travel faster than light?"

"Relativity already determined that no one can travel faster than light," Tamika affirmed.

"What about tachyons?"

"That's a purely hypothetical particle."

I stared at the sunlight cutting through the patio screen, my body levitating in the center of the pool. I gave a slight nod as if I agreed, but my imagination sparked with the possibility. Like Einstein had said, "Imagination is more important than knowledge." And as Tamika had pointed out during my bike-a-thon, "Knowledge is limited, whereas imagination embraces the entire world."

Our scientific debate continued on, covering some of the basic topics like "What if we could break an atom in half, over and over, beyond subatomic particles like strange quarks, until—POOF—it was gone?" and "Since there are billions of rats in the world and only about 500,000 apes, and rodents are just as smart as apes, why wasn't the movie *Planet of the Rats* instead?"

"Okay, how about this," I said, pulling myself out of the water. I wrapped a yellow beach towel around my shivering body and sank into a patio chair. "If all variables are constant with every repeated scenario, is it ever possible to have a different outcome?"

Tamika furrowed her brow. "Of course not. That's the very definition of 'constant.'"

"Well, try to explain that to my mother," I said with a smirk. "She says that two plus two can sometimes equal five."

"Ludicrous," Tamika huffed. "Have you shown her a calculator?"

I nodded so hard, I was sure I looked like a bobble-head. That was literally what I'd done.

"She claims that some people who work with numbers sometimes get *creative*." My fingers made air quotes for added emphasis, exactly as my mom had done.

"Explain."

I shrugged. "My mom just said that you can find the reason in the footnotes."

Would be nice to have access to the footnotes for everything that didn't add up. Like why people moved away and we didn't keep our promise to stay best friends forever. Or why loved ones got sick, and stayed sick even with treatment.

Our conversation once again fell silent, the pool water slapping against the concrete sides as Tamika climbed out. She wrapped herself in a matching towel and settled into the chair next to mine.

Fact: Even though there are tons of black holes in space, scientists say they're just too far away to harm us. I'd always put my faith in the facts. And if at the beginning of the summer someone had said I'd be friends with my nemesis, I'd have said there was a greater chance that Earth would be swallowed by a black hole. Turns out a leopard can change its spots. Not sure, though, which one of us was the leopard.

My mind drifted back to Sir Fig Newton and his slower-than-a-sloth recovery. What if Gran's pastor was right? Maybe despite all the signs, if I weren't afraid and just believed, then Fig would be okay. Dad had said I should be patient, but he didn't have all the facts.

"You know how my cat's sick?"

"I thought he was getting better," she said.

"I used to think so, but now . . ."

I confessed about the barefoot-discovered cat puke and a comatose Fig sleeping past his breakfast head bump. I told her about my parents' solution to Fig's diabetes diagnosis, and how if he needed more tests and additional treatment, my fear was that they'd go back to the original plan and give Sir Fig Newton away.

"I can't imagine my world without Fig."

"This may sound kind of absurd, but"—Tamika leaned in, her face hard and serious—"when things were really awful with my uncle, I survived thanks to my flower."

She picked up her gigantic white flower lying on the patio table. Her hands cradled it as if handling Einstein's original paper on special relativity. "I'm not close with my dad. He travels a lot. And when he's home . . ."

Her voice drifted away as her fingers tugged at the individual petals. "My uncle practically raised me. He took me everywhere. The science center, the movies, the Kennedy Space Center. Right before the first day of kindergarten, I was scared to leave him, so he bought me this. That way he'd always be with me, even when he really wasn't."

Guilt snaked up my spine and coiled around my throat. *That's* where Tamika had gotten her flower? I couldn't stop thinking of how many times I'd made fun of it, calling it silly and weird.

"Whenever things get bad," she continued, "I always have it nearby, reminding me of him. I instantly hear him whistling like he always did while waxing his old pickup. I can feel his beard stubble scratching my cheek when he kissed me good night. It's like he never left."

I nodded. My parents loved me too and would always be there for me. But what if all the money I'd raised ran out and Fig still wasn't better? Maybe Dad would get this new job. And things would finally go back to normal like he'd promised. But what if he didn't? If I couldn't count on my parents, then who could I count on?

A gust of crisp AC air whooshed past as Mrs. Smith opened the sliding glass door. She set a tray with a pitcher of OJ, glass cups, and bowls filled with various fruit and crackers on the patio table.

"What are you two up to?" she asked.

"Talking about Uncle James and the flower he gave me," Tamika said.

"My cat isn't getting better even though I've done everything right," I explained. "I want to believe that everything will be okay, but what if . . ."

Mrs. Smith sighed and sat in one of the patio chairs,

smoothing out the bottom of her sundress. After several silent moments, except for Tamika crunching away on a green apple, she finally spoke.

"After I lost my brother, there was this moment when I completely gave up. I wouldn't answer the phone. I'd ignore emails and texts. I cried for days. And when all the tears were gone, I got angry. I threw away things I cared about. Picked fights with anyone nearby. And then one day I woke up, got dressed, and drove up I-95 with no destination in mind."

Mrs. Smith paused and poured herself a cup of OJ. A slight grin appeared, and her brown eyes brightened.

"Eventually I ended up at a Waffle House. The waitress came to take my order and said, 'What's on your mind, Sunshine?' and I smiled for the first time in weeks. Ever since we were young, James used to say those exact words to me every time I'd get frustrated or down. Somehow right then I just knew I'd be okay."

I snacked on an orange, mulling over Tamika's flower and Mrs. Smith's Waffle House encounter. My back lengthened in my chair as I pictured myself strong like miranium. But what if Fig didn't get better? My body slumped. Familiar words from a stranger or Fig's empty food dish wasn't going to make me feel okay.

I tried digging down to find that extra oomph. But no matter how deep I went, my mind failed. Even if I could travel at the speed of light and go back to that day at the Kennedy Space Center, when life was all good, it wouldn't matter. History would still repeat itself. Life would never be good if Sir Fig Newton wasn't.

✩ 34 ✩

SHORT-CIRCUIT
SCIENTIST

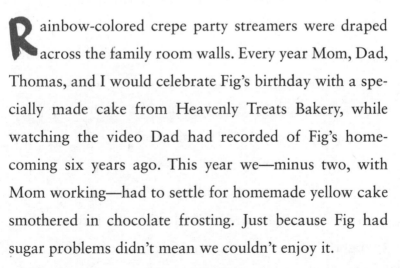

Rainbow-colored crepe party streamers were draped across the family room walls. Every year Mom, Dad, Thomas, and I would celebrate Fig's birthday with a specially made cake from Heavenly Treats Bakery, while watching the video Dad had recorded of Fig's homecoming six years ago. This year we—minus two, with Mom working—had to settle for homemade yellow cake smothered in chocolate frosting. Just because Fig had sugar problems didn't mean we couldn't enjoy it.

"So, I got a second interview."

I gasped and ran over to hug Dad, who had to put down his plate.

Dad laughed. "Okay, okay. Thank you, honey. I'm not getting ahead of myself, but I think I might just get it."

Not only had Dad's funk disappeared ever since my mood-music playlist, but even his cooking skills seemed to have improved. His meat loaf last night wasn't half bad. And this cake was pretty good.

"Everything'll be back to normal in no time."

I wanted to believe Dad's words. I settled back on the couch and ran my hand over Fig's rising belly. He mumbled a satisfied grunt, his paws twitching.

It was the third day in a row that Fig had slept past his breakfast head bump. If only I had something to calm my somersaulting nerves. Something like Tamika's white flower. I pushed my final bite of cake around my plate, creating a swirling chocolate smudge.

"And if you don't get it?" I asked.

"Then I'll get another interview somewhere else, and another, until I get hired," Dad said. His face appeared thoughtful as he shoveled another bite of cake into his mouth. After a few moments he said, "Like your Gran always says, 'God never gives us more than we can handle.'"

I looked at him curiously. "Do you *really* believe in God? You never go to church."

Dad put down his fork. "Of course I do. You don't have to go to church to believe."

We sat there, staring at the video on the TV screen in silence. My six-year-old self cooed over baby Fig pawing at the shoelace Thomas dangled over his head. After a few more moments when the only one talking was my TV persona gushing over the kitty cuteness, I spoke up.

"Gran's pastor said you just have to have faith"— my hand shot out and stroked Fig's gray coat—"and then everything will be okay. But I'm starting to think that's a lie."

"Why would the pastor lie?"

I wanted to lay out the facts, to say that even though I'd raised all that money and Fig was finally getting insulin, he wasn't getting better like he should. But with Dad finally out of his funk, I didn't want to throw another cat-tastrophe at him. Fig curled into a tight ball under my hand.

"You keep saying it's all good, but it's not. This is the worst summer ever. Thomas moved away. My iPhone died. And Fig's got the silent cat killer. Faith is dumb."

Dad's face saddened. "Mira, having faith isn't about *every*thing turning out okay."

"Then what's it about?" I leaned forward.

"Faith is so that *you* will be okay no matter what happens. Whether the something that happens is good or not, nothing lasts forever."

I fell back into the couch, my eyes focused on the TV and a kitten Fig swatting at a jingling ball. The toy bounced across the carpet and rolled under the couch. Kitten Fig's paw swiped under the sofa, but he couldn't reach it. He cried and cried, and finally looked at my young self, then at Thomas for assistance.

"It's tough, Fig Newton, when what you really want is just out of reach," Dad's voice said on the TV.

"I've always got your back, Sir Isaac Newton," my six-year-old self said, rescuing the jingling ball. The real Fig by my side flipped over, exposing his white, furry belly with a whimpering grunt. The video snapped off and a brilliant blue filled the screen.

"One more time," I said.

Fact: Tachyons might be hypothetical, but with a push of a TV remote button, I could travel back in time to when Fig was healthy, Dad had a job, and I was first place in Thomas's life.

I pressed play on the remote. The DVD player whirred and groaned for almost a minute, but the television screen remained blue. The tray popped out on its own and then slid back closed. I smashed the play button again. The machine hummed and rejected the disc once more.

"Check the DVD," Dad said.

I leapt off the couch as the tray launched open again, and I scrambled over to the DVD player. I snatched the disc, scraping it against the plastic as the tray slid shut. My skin prickled. I flipped the disc over and gasped. A deep scratch danced across the shiny surface. Fury jerked through my body. Sir Fig Newton's homecoming video was destroyed.

All hail the Short-Circuit Scientist.

Dad and I sat at the dining table, Fig asleep in a ball at my feet. The smell of garlic, ginger, and sweet-and-sour chicken wafted through the air. I stared at the closed Chinese take-out boxes sitting in the center of the table. Not because I was hungry. My fury might have been squashed thanks to Dad's skills of fixing Fig's DVD with some glass cleaner, cloth, and toothpaste, but the damage was done. I'd been sucked into my own funk.

"Let's give Mom one more minute," Dad said, glancing at the front door. "Then we start without her."

Steam snuck out in twirling swirls from the closed white boxes. Another reminder of how ugly my life was. We couldn't really afford takeout. Dad had gotten it because he'd felt bad about my hysterics over the scratched disc. I might have been sick of mangled meat loaf and puked-up sloppy joes, but Dad's guilt was not the way I wanted to get edible food back in my life.

Silence smothered the room, except for Fig's deep-sleep wheezing. Just as Dad reached for the box with Kung Pao chicken, Mom came bustling through the front door, sending Fig in a crazed scamper toward my room.

"Sorry I'm late, guys," she sighed, kicking off her heels and tossing her suit jacket onto the couch. "I had the worst day. Ripped panty hose, cranky clients, and then the car broke down." Her quick steps slowed to a crawl as she neared the table. "Mr. Chen's?"

Dad stopped scooping white rice onto his plate. "What about the car?"

"I know Mira raised all that money, but don't you think it's a bit premature to get takeout?" Mom said in that exasperated "I've reached my limit" tone.

"It's Fig Newton's birthday," he said matter-of-factly. "Now, what happened to the car?"

Mom slumped into a chair and peeked into the paper containers until she came upon the fried rice. "I thought it was the battery, but the tow truck guy's pretty sure it's the starter."

"Tow truck guy? The starter?" With each echoed word, Dad's face fell into another dimension of disappointment. I silently cursed our disastrous dining table. Never a good idea to sit there.

"Yup. The Toyota's at the repair shop. If he's right, we could be looking at four hundred dollars, minimum." Mom dribbled sauce onto her spring roll and tore into it with such aggression that I jumped in my seat.

This was *not* good at all.

"Why don't we go to church?" I asked.

Her face swung in my direction. "What, honey?"

"Maybe if we did, then Jesus would save Sir Fig Newton, right?" My skin was hot, but my tone was bitter cold. If Jesus could bring a girl back from the dead, he for sure could stop Fig from puking up his guts.

"Sweetie," Mom said, throwing Dad a questioning glance, "what are you talking about? We're following the vet's treatment. I'm sure everything will be—"

"Everything is *not* okay!"

"Mira, enough," Dad said.

"Why don't you believe in God?" I asked Mom.

"I do, honey—"

"Liar!" I slammed my palms on the table, rattling my empty plate.

Dad leapt to his feet. "Mira, go to your room."

"I heard you, Mom." My voice shook. "That night we found out Grandma Millie was in a coma, you said that her accident proves that there's no such thing as God."

Mom reached out for my hand, but I pulled away. She looked like she was about to cry.

"What if there really is a God and because I don't

believe, he's punishing me, and now Jesus will let Sir Fig Newton die?"

I ran to my room and slammed the door shut. I was too mad to cry and too angry to figure out what to do with myself. My fury was back, rushing under my skin with a vengeance.

★✿ 35 ✿★

MAD FAITH IN
EINSTEIN

I paced my bedroom carpet, dodging the pretty-rank clothes pile. My anger fueled my hurried gait and the pounding thought that I would *never* be all good if I lost Fig.

Sir Fig Newton lay on my unmade bed, preening with intense resolve. As I rounded the smelly clothes pile for a third time, Fig paused and stared at me, unblinking. Eventually he yawned, wide enough for me to count all thirty teeth.

I stared back at him. He looked bored with my

relentless pacing. Fig released a heavy sigh, confirming my suspicion. He *was* tired of my frenzied walk.

As my stride relaxed, my panting slowed to a normal twenty breaths per minute.

Fig returned to grooming with a satisfied calm. My anger subsided, and I realized that my outburst at Mom had been over-the-top harsh.

I swallowed hard, guilt tightening my throat. It wasn't fair, attacking Mom like that. With everything gone wrong this summer, the bubbling fear and frustration had finally burst. I desperately wanted her to convince me that everything really would be okay. But how could she? She had no idea what was going on with Fig. None of this was Mom's fault. And all I'd done was hurt her feelings.

Mom entered my room without knocking. I jumped a little but couldn't bring myself to say anything.

I sat on my bed next to Fig, my legs crossed at the ankles. I swung them in anticipation of Mom's punishment. More dish duty? No more hanging out with Tamika?

"Mira." Mom sat next to me, hands folded in her lap. "What's going on?"

SONJA THOMAS

Shocked at her soft voice, I lifted my head. She looked concerned.

Everything spilled out in jumbled relief.

"Fig threw up twice, and for three days in a row he hasn't woken up for breakfast, and Gran's pastor said that if you just believe in God, then everything will be fine, but I don't know if there really is a God, so what if that means Fig won't get better? I don't know what to think, and I'm trying so hard to believe that everything's going to be okay, but my gut keeps telling me otherwise."

Once it all fell out, my body was as light as a feather. But my brain still weighed a ton.

"Fig's throwing up?" Mom reached to squeeze my hand. "Why didn't you tell us?"

"Because . . ." I hesitated. "The last time Fig got a bad diagnosis, you and Dad wanted to give him away."

Mom's face soured as if she'd sucked on a hundred lemons.

"I'm sorry, honey, but your father and I would never *want* to put Sir Fig Newton up for adoption. At the time it just seemed like the only realistic option. We didn't know there was a way to raise all that money. *You* showed us that was possible. It's different now."

"But what if he needs more medicine that costs a hundred times more than the insulin?"

If Sir Fig Newton was taken away from me . . . permanently . . . My insides curdled.

Mom ran her palm over my curls, her face grim. "I'm not going to sugarcoat the situation, Mira. You're already aware that money is tight, and now with the car . . . But even more important, we must consider Fig's quality of life. We have to do what's best for both him and us. And that could mean . . ."

She tried to mask the downward spiral of the conversation with a sympathetic smile, but we both knew what the ultimate outcome could end up being.

I nodded, silently letting her know that she didn't have to say the words.

"But even as awful as everything seems right now, always know that you're not alone in this. Your dad and I love you very much, and we'll do everything we can for Sir Fig Newton, within our means."

Mom stared at her hands resting on her lap. She

flipped them over, clenched them into fists, and slowly reopened them.

"You're right, Mira. I don't really believe in God."

I looked up at her, eyes wide.

"But I never wanted my beliefs to influence you. I want you to come to your own conclusions. And regardless of whether there is a God, I'm sure he would *never* punish you by letting Fig die. I'm sure he'd love you. Everybody loves you."

I managed a small smile, but the fear and frustration still stuck to my skin.

"Losing grandma was incredibly hard," she continued, "but now I understand that nothing lasts forever. Everything, joy and pain, will pass."

I nodded and bit my lip. "I'm sorry, Mom. For today and also for when I said I wish we could give you away instead. I didn't mean it."

Mom's head tilted to the side, her thick red hair spilling past her shoulders. "I know, sweetheart. I know. Just remember that you, me, and Dad are strong. Superstrong. Together we can face anything and make it through to the other side."

Mom pulled me into her lap and wrapped her arms tight around me. I caught a whiff of her fading lavender perfume and the fried rice from dinner. I tried snuggling into her, but my elbows poked out and my knees just wouldn't fit. I wished I were younger and still believed in Santa Claus and the tooth fairy, young enough for Mom's hugs to swallow away my fears and doubts and fill me up with courage, calm, and strength.

Unfortunately, I'd grown up.

The setting sun cast a bright spotlight across my bedroom wall. I lay on my bed, my arms and legs splayed out like a star. Fig was snoozing on my belly. I could tell he was in a deep sleep because his full weight squashed into my intestines like a five-hundred-pound dumbbell.

Turned out the tow truck guy was right and my parents' car was going to cost them a supermassive amount of money. And Dad was still waiting to find out if he got the job or not. I rested my palm on Fig, comforted by the steady rise and fall of his tummy. Thank Einstein I'd raised all that money. It was the only reason my parents had agreed to the additional testing at the vet yesterday to find out why Fig was still sick. Now we just had to wait for the results.

My eyelids closed. Long pauses dragged between Fig's deep breaths, our bellies rising and falling in sync. My thoughts sprinted back to the comfort I'd felt at the Operation Save Fig bike-a-thon. I thought about all the people who had cheered me on: my parents, Gran, Mrs. B, and so many others. And, of course, Tamika.

The nickname "Miranium" fit because I *was* strong, not because I was made of the toughest, strongest, most indestructible element ever. I was strong because I fought for what I believed in and I never gave up. I was strong because I was supported by family, friends, and even strangers. I'd dug down deep, and that extra oomph had found me.

My eyes fluttered open. Fig was still on my belly. I stroked Fig's gray coat, and his body vibrated with his purrs.

"Everyone wants you to get well and kick this cat killer to the curb," I murmured.

Suddenly Sir Fig Newton jumped up onto all fours, his claws digging through my shirt and clamping into my skin.

"Ouch!" I yelped.

His eyes wide, he leapt onto the floor. His body writhed, and the most disturbing retching sounds poured out of his gaping jaws. I flinched. My instinct was to hold him tight and make the torture go away. But I was afraid to touch him. His body continued to contort in violent spasms. The seconds slithered forward until Fig's dinner splattered onto the carpet in a pile of brownish sludge.

Fig scurried to the other side of the room and plopped onto the fold-and-put-away pile. Within a microsecond he was snoring. A sour stench lingered in the air.

After cleaning up, I gazed at Fig's sleeping body. I waited. And watched. And waited some more.

"Don't . . . don't leave me." My voice cracked. I snatched my gaze away.

I slunk toward my bed, paused at my dresser, and stared at the altered photo from the day at the Kennedy Space Center. Fig looked so content, snuggled in my arms. It was a flash moment in time, when everything had been all good: Dad had had his job, Mom had dressed in her *Star Trek* costume, and Thomas had been standing by my side. The evidence, however, was gone—

319

cut up and thrown away, just like my hope. I needed something bigger to help.

Maybe faith was like Einstein with all his theories—ideas with no proof. Einstein hadn't been afraid to share his theories, and he'd definitely believed in them. Some had been proven during his lifetime, others long after he was gone. And sometimes he'd been wrong. But that's okay too.

I wasn't convinced there was a God, and I had no firm hypothesis on what happened to us after we died, but I did have mad faith in one person. I picked up my Einstein-in-a-lab-coat piggy bank and stared at it. Couldn't hurt having a conversation, right? Just one creative genius talking to another.

"Hey, Einstein," I whispered down to that mess of white hair, "if you're out there somewhere and you can hear me, then please, help everything be okay. For me, for Mom and Dad, but especially for Sir Fig Newton. Thanks."

36

SAY IT ISN'T SOY

Fact: Dark matter is completely invisible and can be found EVERYWHERE. It's what scientists believe holds the Milky Way and all other galaxies together, kind of like a giant spiderweb. Some scientists believe dark matter doesn't really exist. But something I couldn't see or understand was holding me together so that I didn't completely break and stop working, like my cell phone at the beginning of summer.

The vet had called with the additional test results: inconclusive. Sir Fig Newton had no more oomph, and I

321

was starting to feel the same. The hydrogen, carbon dioxide, and methane in my gut churned. Even though I was strong like miranium, I was more scared than ever.

I huddled in my bed, watching Fig snooze. The day after tomorrow I was supposed to go with Tamika to the Orlando Science Center.

Bleh. So what.

If Mrs. Smith hadn't already purchased the tickets two weeks ago when I'd accepted the invitation, I'd have made up an excuse now to not go.

Dr. Spires had recommended even more tests for Fig, which my parents had said we'd consider, but for now we would follow his other suggestion to "wait and see." It didn't look good. Almost every day this past week, Fig had slept way past breakfast. And to top that off, last night after Fig's dinner there was another throw-up incident.

My cramped gut felt like puking too. The black hole had won. It had finally pulled me in.

Suddenly the doorbell rang. Fig didn't budge. I curled into a tighter ball. The doorbell chimed again: three quick, shrill buzzes. A minute later there was a knock at my door.

"Yeah?"

Dad poked his head in. "Sorry, Mira girl, but Tamika's here."

Oh. I'd forgotten that we'd planned on hanging out today.

"I can tell her to come another time if you want," Dad said softly.

I slid off the bed. "No, I can face my own battles."

As I slogged down the hall, my mind checked through a list of excuses for why I couldn't hang out. Tamika's smile faded as I approached. She'd had the same look of concern on the day she'd given me her uncle's magic elixir. Orange juice couldn't cure me now.

"Are you okay?" she asked.

All my excuses vanished, and I broke open. I shared every detail with Tamika, from Sir Fig Newton's no more oomph to the inconclusive test results.

"I don't know what else to do. I've faced the facts, and I don't like them."

After I was done, she nodded slowly. She touched the white flower behind her ear, the one from her uncle, and wrapped me in a tight hug. I exhaled.

With Fig still sick, the black hole was strong. But Tamika reminded me I wasn't alone. With my family and friends, I was stronger. My oomph was inching its way back. And with my persistence that crummy black hole would eventually shrink and no longer have such a strong gravitational pull.

I hugged Tamika back.

An hour passed with Tamika in my room. My heart rate finally elevated slightly above somber territory as we engaged in a heated debate over which came first, the chicken or the egg.

"So obvious," Tamika said, straightening her white flower. "Egg-laying animals like turtles and gators existed way before chickens. Therefore, eggs came first."

She relaxed into my desk chair with a grin.

"But wait." I held up my finger, ready to poke holes in her theory. "Everyone knows that the question doesn't mean any old egg. Did the chicken or the *chicken egg* come first?"

Tamika huffed, her air of supremacy leaking out.

"Not so obvious, is it?" Finally my turn to be smug.

"Team *chicken* egg all the way because—"

My bedroom door swung open, paralyzing Tamika's rant. My dad strolled in with a tray topped with two soda cans and a plate of cookies. Fig lifted his head with barely opened eyes and then promptly settled back down to nap.

"Thought I'd bring you girls a snack." Dad set the tray on my desk.

"Wait!" I cried as Tamika's hand shot out and snatched a cookie. I sprang off my bed and smacked the baked not-so-good out of her hand before it could touch her tongue.

"Mira?" Dad asked, looking confused.

"I, uh . . ." There was no sugarcoating the fact that Dad's skills in the kitchen were the equivalent of mine at keeping a clean room.

Then it hit me. "What's in this? Tamika's allergic to nuts and dairy."

Dad's face restored, he nodded. "I call them Nacho Crunch. No nuts and no dairy."

"Nacho Crunch cookies?" That didn't tempt my taste buds.

"Yup," he said, wiggling his brows. "My own creation

325

with a secret ingredient. Especially made for my number one daughter and her friend."

"Thanks, Dad," I said, pushing him out of my room and closing the door.

"Wait." I rushed at Tamika again, wanting to spare her the misery of Dad's cuisine. But before I could take one full stride, she'd shoved the cookie into her mouth and gobbled it up.

"Wow," she said, wiping the crumbs from her face. "That was delicious."

Either this girl had faulty taste buds or she really was an odd, evil scientist. I might need to rethink this friendship. She plucked another cookie off the plate and inhaled it like Sir Fig Newton used to do with his meals.

I hated to admit it, but I was intrigued. I moseyed toward my desk and lightly picked up a cookie, afraid that its very touch might bruise my skin. When I raised it to my parted lips, odd spices struck my nose: chili, paprika, and cumin. With my eyes squeezed shut, I nibbled and swallowed.

Crunchy tomato flavor with taco seasonings. Tamika was right. It *was* delicious. This was a Guinness World

Record moment. Dad had made something 100 percent yummy.

"All righty, Miss Know-It-All," Tamika said, and smirked, "what came first—the chicken or the *chicken* egg?"

We resumed our debate, a battle to the death, with sharp scientific evidence to support our chosen theory—Tamika, Team Egg, and me, Team Chicken. Not even twenty minutes had passed after we'd scarfed down the entire plate of cookies, when Tamika's gut interrupted my explanation of mutations in DNA over thousands of generations to create a new species. The sound wasn't your normal hungry growl. It was more like a monster deep in the bowels of her belly, roaring and clawing to get out.

"Are you okay?" I inched toward her.

Moaning, Tamika doubled over. I touched her shoulder. She flinched. The gurgling began to surface, growing louder and deeper, with fewer pauses in between. Tamika looked up at me, sweat and tears streaming down her face.

"Bathroom?" she managed to squeak.

"First door on your left." I pointed toward my bedroom door.

Holding her stomach, she scampered into the hall. Seconds later a door slammed.

Something furry brushed against my leg. Fig looked up at me with wanting eyes. I bent down and scratched his scruff, then gave him a fingernail massage up and down his back. His lean front legs stretched forward, and his backside shot into the air, making an in-your-face butt scratch demand.

"Today's been rough," I sighed, heeding Fig's request.

I paused, straining to hear any SOS calls. "That's the kind of response I expect from Dad's usual dishes. I don't understand what happened. He said there were no nuts or dairy."

Sir Fig Newton circled around, guiding my hand to the appropriate scratching spots. "Nacho Crunch sounds gross for a cookie, but I'm fine. It would make a great name for a ch—"

I sucked in my breath.

"Dad!" I tore down the hall.

"Dad!" Past the living and dining rooms.

"Dad!" I skidded to a stop in the family room, almost slamming into his tall, wiry frame.

"Mira, what's wrong?"

"What's the secret ingredient?"

"What?"

"Nacho Crunch. Tamika's really sick. What did you put in it?"

"Oh no." Dad's face crumbled. "Um, onion, garlic powder—"

"No. The secret ingredient."

He sheepishly grinned. "Doritos."

"But, Dad," I said, "Doritos have *dairy* in them."

"Oh." His body sagged.

Wait. I was onto something big here, I knew it. I squeezed my eyes shut and thought about all my evidence. Doritos had caused Tamika to vomit. . . . Fig was vomiting . . . and it was always right after he ate his fancy diabetes food. . . .

Big bang! If Tamika could have such a violent stomach-churning reaction, then maybe, just maybe, Fig had suffered the same cause and effect.

I opened my eyes. "Come with me." I grabbed Dad's

hand and dragged him to the kitchen. I glanced at the oven clock. The digits read 4:46. I poured OJ into a tall glass and shoved it into his hand. "Give this to Tamika. I need to make a quick call before it's too late."

Dad eyed me, then the glass curiously, but didn't protest. He shuffled down the hall toward my room.

I snatched the phone from the wall. My fingers punched the keypad seven times. As I twirled the spiral phone cord tight around my finger, my confidence thinned with each ring. Less than fifteen minutes before they closed.

"Brevard Animal Clinic," a sugarcoated voice sing-songed.

"Mira Williams calling for Dr. Spires," I said as urgently as I could.

"One moment please."

Instrumental jazz buzzed in my ear, sending my current stress level to a 6.9. I did a quick pulse check. Definitely over one hundred rapid beats per minute.

"Dr. Spires is just finishing up with a furry patient," the voice said, drowning in syrupy-sweet kindness. "Would you like to hold or have him call you back?"

"I'll wait."

The hold music snapped back on, this time a classical piece. With each pound of the piano keys, a sharp stab was driven through my chest. My heartbeat quickened, my stress levels surpassing total destruction on the Richter scale.

"Hello, hello, Mira," a familiar voice said. "How's everything with Sir Fig Newton?"

"Well, I told you last time how Fig keeps throwing up, right?"

"Right."

"But today I realized it always happens after he eats. Could he possibly be allergic to the new food?"

"Hmm . . ." I could practically feel Dr. Spires's mustache twitch. "Remind me which brand of diabetic food he's on?"

I rushed to the cupboard, the spiral phone cord stretched flat, and read the name from the bag.

"Give me a moment."

The instrumental torture kicked back on. I resumed twisting the cord around my finger. The pause was long. The phone cord wound around my hand, making its way up my arm toward my elbow. Next stop, my throat.

Finally an "Okay, okay" disturbed the silence.

"Let's take a look, shall we? Poultry by-product meal, soy protein isolate, corn gluten meal, soy flour . . ."

There was another pause. My nerves twisted.

"There's a possibility Sir Fig Newton has an allergy to one of these common ingredients," Dr. Spires said. "Chicken, corn, wheat, and soy can sometimes trigger food sensitivities in cats."

My nerves and the phone cord unfurled.

"We'll switch him to wet food and see if that makes a difference. You know, your dad's right, Mira." Dr. Spires chuckled. "You are an amazing girl."

My cheeks exploded with heat.

The phone safe in its cradle, my mood was zooming toward turbulence-free skies. Now if only I could accelerate forward and have Fig already on allergen-free food. I hustled to my bedroom and found Dad hovering over Tamika. She sat cross-legged on my bed, cradling the full glass of OJ. Her body shivered as if the president had declared an immediate end to NASA and all space exploration.

Dad and I locked worried gazes. My eyes darted to

Tamika, then back to Dad, questioning if she was all right. Dad nodded. He reached out toward her shoulder, but pulled back before making contact. He shuffled toward the door and paused in front me. Ruffling my curls, he mouthed the words "I'm sorry" and slunk out of the room.

"Tamika?" I tiptoed in her direction, not sure what to say or do. My dad had practically poisoned her, twisting her guts into an explosive device.

She slurped her drink, her eyes averted from me.

"I'm really, really sorry."

Silence.

"Are you feeling better?"

Her head snapped up with a death-stare. I shuddered.

"It's all my fault," I said. "I should've warned my dad about Doritos. He didn't know they have dairy in them, but come on, Nacho Crunch cookies? Who'd have thunk?"

I smiled awkwardly, hoping Tamika would forgive me. I caught her face softening before her head hung back down and she stared into her empty glass.

"It's not your fault," she said. "I realized after eating

the cookies what the secret ingredient was, but I—I didn't say anything. I guess I was kind of hoping that maybe *this* time it wouldn't affect me, and maybe by not acknowledging it, nothing bad would happen."

"But it's not all bad."

Tamika's head lifted and our eyes met, her face a smashed-up combo of curiosity and perturbation. "Elaborate."

"You may have just saved Sir Fig Newton's life."

Her stare turned to Fig snoozing at the opposite end of the bed.

I caught Tamika up to speed, regurgitating my phone conversation with Dr. Spires about the possible food allergy. "It could be chicken, corn, wheat, or soy."

Tamika smiled big. "I'm glad everything's going to be all right, *El*mira."

My nose scrunched as if assaulted by Fig's pungent puke. I decided to finally address a matter that had burned my patience for years.

"Why do you always call me 'Elmira,' extra emphasis on the first syllable, when you know I go by 'Mira'?"

She furrowed her brow in confusion. "What do you

mean? It's like in Spanish, how all words are feminine or masculine."

"But '*el*' is masculine," I said, frowning.

"Right. El Mira. It sounds commanding. Regal. Like '*el presidente*.' You know, strong, like you." Tamika smiled. "The one and only Mira."

My burning cheeks stretched into a huge grin.

37

OVER THE MOON

Tamika and I climbed the stairs to the second level of the Orlando Science Center, headed to the *Journey to Space* traveling exhibit. My pulse was racing with excitement.

Fact: For the first time all summer, everything was *really* all good.

Dad had gotten the job—the same one he'd interviewed for right after listening to his made-for-him playlist by his number one daughter. Mom had applied for a part-time job at the community theater. And we'd switched Sir Fig

Newton to wet diabetic food. My fingers were crossed that he'd make a speedy recovery.

Laughter, shrieks, and conversations echoed in the large hall. The walls and high ceiling, both painted black, added to the illusion of boundless space. Feet pounded against the cement floor as kids and parents ventured among seven areas, exploring different aspects of life in space, learning about the challenges of space travel, and imagining a future where Earth was not the only planet humans called home.

Mrs. Smith had dropped us off and had gone to spend a few hours treating herself to "retail therapy" at the Fashion Square Mall. During the hour drive to the museum, Tamika and I had chatted and giggled nonstop. We'd talked about everything, from two NASA astronauts performing the first female spacewalk with an all-female crew later this year, to the first day of seventh grade happening the day after tomorrow.

We wandered over to the first area—Space Is Dangerous—and watched a video of a hole being blown through a thick metal plate by a simulated meteoroid. Feeling energized, I impulsively hugged Tamika during the slow-motion impact.

I was over the moon to be here.

"This exhibit is astounding!" Tamika said, her smile as big as the white flower tucked behind her ear.

We dashed toward a display featuring a pair of Neil Armstrong's gloves worn during his *Apollo 11* mission. The next case housed a Canyon Diablo meteorite, one of many fragments of the asteroid that created the Barringer Meteor Crater in Arizona. The meteor hit approximately fifty thousand years ago and weighed several hundred thousand tons!

I nodded toward an X-ray of a full space suit. "Hey, it's free." We hurried over and eagerly read about the many features that protected astronauts against the extreme temperatures and radiation.

As we made our way through all seven areas, we encountered a ton of awesome interactive displays. We launched water rockets, tested gravity in a drop tower, and controlled a robotic arm. We even got to sit on a full-sized mock-up of a toilet that astronauts used in space.

After hurrying past a bunch of screaming kids playing with a dollhouse-sized space station, we arrived at my favorite part of the exhibit, the Rotating Destiny Lab. It looked just like the real International Space Station's US Destiny Laboratory module, which I'd seen many times on the NASA website.

The moment we entered, a spotlight took turns highlighting each piece of equipment on the racks of the curved walls, while a narrator's voice gave a detailed description. We stood on a platform with the module slowly rotating around us. It felt like I was floating in space!

In the last area of the exhibit, Tamika and I stood behind adult-sized astronaut suits, our faces peering through space helmets. Behind us was a huge backdrop of the Red Planet, Mars. A museum employee stood in front of us, holding up Tamika's cell phone. "Say 'cheese'!"

At the exact same time, Tamika and I shouted, "Provolone!" and busted into hysterics.

Smiling big, I thought about how two years ago we'd both been here for our fifth-grade field trip. I'd spent the entire time by Thomas's side. I couldn't even picture Tamika in that group, hanging out with our classmates. We'd learned about astronomy: stuff like gravity, sound

SONJA THOMAS

waves, and space warps. The best was when Thomas collapsed to the ground and joked that he'd *fallen into a black hole and could never get out*. Even though the memory caused my usual snort-giggle reaction, I could only picture being with Tamika here now.

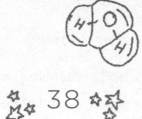

38

AFTER EINSTEIN, OF COURSE

A high-pitched "MAOW!" stabbed my eardrums. My eyes flew open and zeroed in on the glowing digits of my alarm clock. 5:41 a.m. There had been a time when I'd loathed such rude awakenings. Now, however, I greeted Sir Fig Newton's head bump with a joyous scratch behind his ear.

We headed to the kitchen, Fig leading the way. I filled a disposable syringe with the three-units dosage and set it aside. I pulled up the tab on a can of diabetic wet food and yanked the metal top off with the familiar *whoosh*, causing Fig to "mrow" repeatedly. I placed his full food dish on the feeding mat at the end of the elaborate obstacle course.

Fig leapt onto the kitchen table and dutifully dashed across the wood into the tunnel. The polyester crinkled with each step as he zoomed through the tube. Then he landed at the base of the three-story cat tower. He sprang up to each level with ease until he reached the top.

And just like every other morning over the past month, Sir Fig Newton inhaled the entire bowl in thirty seconds flat, then followed with a frozen pause and a low rumbling, "Urp."

I picked up the syringe, grasped a fold of Fig's flesh high on the neck, and pinched firmly, tenting the skin. Now that I was in seventh grade, Dad had said I was old enough to handle the insulin duties. I think he was just happy to push the responsibility off onto me. With Mom's permission, of course.

I pushed the plunger with my thumb and withdrew the needle, all in one smooth, quick microsecond. After replacing the orange cap over the needle, I dropped the used syringe into a dedicated recycle bin that would be dropped off at the vet when full. Fig rubbed up against my leg, his white-tipped tail waving in a satisfied "Hip Hop Hooray" motion.

Fact: Curiosity and persistence saved the cat.

After a tasty breakfast of scrambled eggs, bacon, and toast, made by Mom, and tea and hot cocoa with marsh-mallows, made by Dad, I headed back to my room. Tamika was coming over later and we were going to brainstorm possible experiments for our YouTube channel, *Science Rocks*, hosted by the two greatest scientists in the universe, after Einstein, of course.

Knowing that every great scientist needed a spark of inspiration, I opened my book *101 Kids' Super Fun Science Experiments*. Sitting on my dresser next to the book, three pictures snatched my attention. One was a framed photo of Tamika and me at the Orlando Science Center, looking as if we were astronauts exploring the Red Planet. The second photo was of Tamika, Becky, Poppy, and me all wearing the Team Apptitude shirts made for my bike-a-thon. We were posing in front of the Spaceship Earth geosphere at Epcot for my thirteenth birthday. To the right was the picture of Sir Fig Newton snuggled in my arms at the Kennedy Space Center, the nose of the shuttle *Atlantis* still visible.

My parents and Thomas, however, had been erased from the scene.

I thought about that day with Thomas, when we'd been staring at the portraits of space heroes and legends in the US Astronaut Hall of Fame. "That'll be you up there someday, Miranium," he'd said to me.

I put the book back on the dresser and released a heavy sigh. I'd accepted a long time ago that Thomas and I were no longer best friends. But I'd finally realized that our friendship fading was okay. It was just like when a binary star—two stars going around the same point—grows farther apart. Their gravitational bond weakens, so that when another star passes the binary, the pair break up.

I settled at my desk and logged into my email account on my new tablet. I opened the email Thomas had sent last week. It was the first time we'd had contact in over two months, since our phone call he'd cut short to hang out with Pete.

From: Thomas Thompson

To: Mira Williams

Date: Oct 4, 6:36 AM

Subject: Knock, knock

> Knock, knock.
>
> Who's there?
>
> Abby.
>
> Abby who?
>
> Abby birthday to you.
>
> Thomas

When I'd first seen his email, I'd been shocked. I'd read it over and over but had never replied. I didn't know what to say. Mom and Dad were right. Nothing lasts forever. But no longer being best friends didn't make us enemies.

I hit the reply button. My eyes danced over the blank screen. Taking a deep breath, I began to type.

From: Mira Williams

To: Thomas Thompson

Date: Oct 12, 7:56 AM

Subject: RE: Knock, knock

Hey, Thomas!

Thanks for the birthday wishes. So much has happened and I want to share it all with you.

Seventh grade is really great, except I have PE first period. What's the point of even taking a shower before school? I'm treasurer of the science club and this year is the year I *will* win the science fair. I also entered NASA's Name the Rover contest. If my essay wins, then the new Mars rover that launches next year will be called Persistence!

My dad got a new job, thank Einstein. My stomach couldn't handle any more sloppy regurgitated joes. And my mom's back to trying on different personas. This week she's Supreme Court Justice Ruth Bader Ginsburg!

You're never going to believe this, but remember my nemesis, Tamika Smith? We are actually the best of friends. Once you get past the smarter-than-thou attitude, she's really not that bad.

Thanks to her nacho chip allergy, Sir Fig Newton is

allllllllllllllladjkasdfqjwiofqkw,z

A furry blur had leapt onto my desk and plopped down right onto my tablet.

"Fig!"

He ignored me and lovingly licked his paw. I snatched a pen from my WORLD'S GREATEST SCIENTIST cup and scratched the capped end into the fur above his tail. His backside twitched, but his attention remained glued to picking away at his claw jam. I flicked my pen from side to side, each end taking turns smacking against the desktop.

Thunk-thunk-thunk.

Fig's ears snapped back. He released a low hiss and swiped at my pen. I waved it back and forth, raising it out of reach. Fig sprung onto his paws, his gaze never wavering from his target. I tossed it across the room—Sir Fig Newton scrambled off my desk after it—and it bounced off my ever-growing pile of smells-pretty-rank laundry.

I read over the email and giggled at the nonsensical

paragraph of letters and numbers and symbols at the end, courtesy of Fig's rump.

This past summer my entire family had been sucked into a black hole with no hope of escape. Losing Thomas and almost losing Fig had torn me in two. But maybe black holes weren't the monsters we made them out to be. Maybe they didn't really want to swallow us whole. Maybe the darkness wanted us to be still and see the universe from a different point of view. It only felt like being spaghettified because the more we tried to avoid the pain, the more it stretched, twisted, and burned, trying to get our attention.

I couldn't blame the end of our friendship on Thomas choosing Pete over me. Even when Thomas had still been reaching out, I had pushed him away. I'd been so wound up with everything going on with Fig that I'd refused his call and ignored his emails. As weird as it sounds, I'm glad Tamika moved into his old house when she did. I know I'll be okay without him. And now that Thomas has Pete, it's good to know he'll be okay without me.

I hit delete on my tablet and started again.

From: Mira Williams

To: Thomas Thompson

Date: Oct 12, 8:01 AM

Subject: RE: Knock, knock

Thomas,

Thanks for the birthday joke. So much has happened.

Things got really bad with Sir Fig Newton. I was really scared and I wished that I could go back in time, to before summer, when you were still here and Fig was fine. It hurt when you started hanging out with Pete. It made me mad that everything was OK with you when my life was so messy. But then I realized that being so far apart, it made sense that we both had found new friends.

Thank Einstein, Fig's blood sugar is back in check. He's lean and healthy and has as much energy as the Magic's center going up and down the court.

Even though we may never hang out again, I

just want you to know that I miss you and I hope

that you're happy in DC.

Mira

I reread the email and hit send. It didn't matter if Thomas wrote back or not. No matter what, we would always be friends.

After a quick shower I hurried to the kitchen, Fig shadowing my lead. Tamika would be at my house any minute. I'd been shocked to learn that she'd never seen a plasma ball in the microwave, so I wanted to surprise her with my grape experiment—with Mom supervising, of course—before we focused on our science vlog. And maybe with Tamika's help, I wouldn't short-circuit everything.

It wasn't that long ago that I'd referred to my nemesis as an annoying evil scientist. Now Tamika was a permanent element in my life and we were no longer brutal competitors. Together we'd convinced the science club to join the Galaxy Zoo project to help scientists classify galaxies. We were even collaborating with other students to host our school's first Earth Day celebration, where students could share their concerns and brainstorm ideas to help make a difference in our community.

Tamika was my best friend.

Although I still planned on winning first place at the science fair this year, we pinky swore we'd help each other with our individual projects. I could definitely use some pointers on giving an outstanding oral presentation. And, of course, I was the queen of research and persistence. Fellow scientists should always stick together.

I'd decided that for this year's fair I was going to do my mood-music project, the same one that had helped my dad out of his funk and was the lucky charm that had gotten him his job.

Of course, I'd have at least twenty test subjects this time, but I was also thinking of building a mood-music app. Poppy had already promised to help me if I did. That way, during the fair everyone could test out my hypothesis that music could change one's mood. It wasn't just about the number of heartbeats per minute, but about the personal connections. Like Mrs. B crying happy tears when she heard the song from her sister's wedding. Or whenever P-Funk played and I couldn't stop grinning because it reminded me of Dad and his silly dancing.

I wanted to show that an experiment wasn't just about the facts, that it could really mean something.

Up until this summer, I'd only had faith in the facts. But after everything that had happened with my parents, Thomas, Tamika, and Sir Fig Newton, I realized that it's okay to believe in something unknown, something bigger than myself. Like Gran had said, faith allows for possibilities.

I fetched a bag of green grapes from the fridge and placed it on the countertop, alongside a knife and plate. Sir Fig Newton sat at attention on the kitchen floor. I inhaled deeply. Mom's blueberry muffins were baking in the oven.

"We did it, Fig. We survived the worst summer ever."

Fig chattered, his excitement matching mine.

Fact: Grapes don't always explode with scientific reliability. I was certain, however, that even if the world kept throwing scary stuff at me, it was all good. No matter what, I'd be okay. I had the same four qualities as any great scientist: I was patient, curious, observant, and persistent. I was Miranium, the strongest element in the universe.

ACKNOWLEDGMENTS

Writing acknowledgments for my debut novel, I feel like a first-time winner at the Oscars (or better yet, the Grammys). Thankfully the orchestra won't cut in to boot me off the stage, but I'll try my best to not ramble on too long (fingers crossed).

To start, thank you so much to my wonderful agent, Ronald Gerber. You saw something in *Sir Fig Newton* and believed in my writing, and for that I'm forever grateful. Thank you for your amazing editorial eye and unwavering support.

Thank you to my brilliant editor, Aly Heller. Your immediate love of Mira and Sir Fig filled my heart with such joy and I'm in awe of how you continually bring out the best in my writing while staying true to the story. I'm so grateful for your collaboration and dedication to bringing Mira and Sir Fig Newton into the world.

And a huge thank you to the rest of the incredible team behind this book at Aladdin/S&S, especially Valerie Garfield, Kristin Gilson, Elizabeth Mims, Olivia Ritchie, Tiara Iandiorio, and Sara Berko. And another huge thanks to copy editors extraordinaire Bara MacNeill and Chloe Kuka, and to the incredibly talented Brittney Bond for illustrating the most adorable cover, featuring a persistent biracial Black girl and her chonky cat.

I wouldn't be realizing this dream if it wasn't for my amazing writing community. Whether giving critiques, advice, mentorship, encouragement, or a good laugh when I needed it most, thank you, thank you, thank you to Vanessa McClelland, Carolyn O'Doherty, Kelly Garrett, Mark McCarron-Fraser, Curtis Chen, Fonda Lee, Robin Herrera, Miriam Forster, Kristina Martin, Christina Struyk-Bonn, Joe Morreale, Paul McKlendin, Emily Eldred, Susan Shreve, Kathleen Muldoon, David Greenberg, Susan Blackaby, Bill Cameron, Eric Kimmel, Cat Winters, Jenn Reese, Lisa Schroeder, my #22Debuts

I would also like to thank Literary Arts and judge David-Matthew Barnes for recognizing Mira and Sir Fig Newton early on with the 2016 OLA Fellowship: the Edna L. Holmes Fellowship in Young Readers Literature. This lit the fire that had me diving back into my manuscript revisions and eventually querying and signing with my awesome agent.

Last, but certainly most important, are my family and friends. Thank you so much for cheering me on and believing in me when I was ready to give up (again and again). There are so many of you who have supported me along this very long journey, so it's impossible to give a shout-out to everyone individually, but know that I am so grateful that you've been a part of my life. A special heartfelt thanks to Jeannette Lancien, Dawn Loehlein, Lisa Nabipour, Jin Park, Elena Carrington, Monique White, Alicia Powers, my friends from GG&D, Common Cause, NACHC, and Powell's Books, editorial cats Gabbie Lu and Brutus, and my fur babies Whiskey and Bailey. And so much love to my brother, Fred Thomas, my sis-in-law,

Libby Rejman, and my beautiful mother, Lydia Thomas.

Mom, thank you for always supporting my dream, even when it made you worry or when you didn't always like what I had written. You embody everything I strive to be: full of joy, love, smiles, patience, honesty, and empathy. Thank you for always making me feel loved and seen. I love you times infinity.

ABOUT THE AUTHOR

Sonja Thomas writes stories for readers of all ages, often featuring brave everyday girls doing extraordinary things. *Sir Fig Newton and the Science of Persistence* is her debut novel. She's a contributing author for *Good Night Stories for Rebel Girls: 100 Real-Life Tales of Black Girl Magic* and was the recipient of the 2016 Oregon Literary Arts Edna L. Holmes Fellowship in Young Readers. Raised in Central Florida and a Washington, DC, transplant for eleven years, she's now "keeping it weird" in the Pacific Northwest. Visit her online at BySonjaThomas.com.